03

LOVE IN HIDING

LOVE IN HIDING

Helen McCabe

Chivers Press • **G.K. Hall & Co.**
Bath, England   **Waterville, Maine USA**

This Large Print edition is published by Chivers Press, England, and by G.K. Hall & Co., USA.

Published in 2001 in the U.K. by arrangement with D.C. Thomson & Co. Ltd.

Published in 2001 in the U.S. by arrangement with Helen McCabe.

U.K. Hardcover ISBN 0-7540-4556-0 (Chivers Large Print)
U.K. Softcover ISBN 0-7540-4557-9 (Camden Large Print)
U.S. Softcover ISBN 0-7838-9482-1 (Nightingale Series Edition)

The text of this Large Print edition is unabridged.
Other aspects of the book may vary from the original edition.

Set in 16 pt. New Times Roman.

Printed in Great Britain on acid-free paper.

British Library Cataloguing in Publication Data available

Library of Congress Cataloging-in-Publication Data

McCabe, Helen, 1942–
    Love in hiding / by Helen McCabe.
        p. cm.
    ISBN 0-7838-9482-1 (lg. print : sc : alk. paper)
    1. Large type books. I. Title.
    PR6113.C35 L68 2001
    823'.92—dc21   2001024197

CHAPTER ONE

'Alys, do stand still, my dear, and try not to slouch!' Lady Margaret Symons ordered. 'You have such a pretty head and shoulders!'

Alys Symons sighed but, nevertheless, stood obediently, while her maid, Abigail, fiddled with the starched ruff. She must do what her lady mother said, but she would have rather been running free through the gardens, dressed in her shift, like any common girl on their estate. The whole of her young body ached, by the end of each day, in the tight-laced prison of her whalebone corset.

'Yes, Mother,' she murmured.

She allowed Abby to try on the uncomfortable ruff which, because Alys was as yet unmarried, was only made to fit as far forward as the shoulders. It had been starched and caused Alys's neck to rub red and sore, every time she wore it. Added to this, today, she had to suffer from a farthingale, a wire cage which spread out her sky-blue skirts to ridiculous proportions!

'How long will this nonsense last?' Alys muttered under her breath.

She was a spirited girl, who wanted to fly like a young swallow and be free from the horrors of lacing and uncomfortable ruffs! And she would have to change again for the feast this evening.

'What did you say, child?' her mother asked.

She was looking unusually regal in plum-coloured velvet instead of her sober black day dress.

'Nothing of importance, my lady!' Alys replied and fidgeted while Abigail pinched her neck unmercifully. 'Oh, Abby, be careful!'

Lady Symons looked up sharply as her daughter raised her voice and, suddenly, Alys felt daring and determined enough to question her, even though her mother was sure to scold her and say it was rude to pry.

'Why must I be dressed up this afternoon, Mother? I don't like it.'

Although her father was due home from Court, he would not care what finery she wore. He loved her for herself, and she loved him dearly. He always made much fuss of her, which was more than her mother did. He denied her nothing. Alys knew that he mourned greatly the loss of her baby brother, James, who had died at just one year old and that he was fearful of losing her, too. She wanted to please her father always, but her mother was made of much sterner stuff and was staring keenly at Alys now, as if, suddenly, she hardly recognised her.

Strangely enough, instead of telling her off for her impertinence, Lady Symons smiled bleakly at her wayward daughter.

'You must always look like a lady, Alys. It is

your duty.'

The slight smile suited Lady Symons. She was a handsome woman, who had borne five ailing children, four boys and just one girl, the sole survivor, Alys, who looked far from weakly now, with her roses and cream complexion and sparkling, mischievous blue eyes.

'You know your father rides home from Court this evening,' she added.

Alys nodded impatiently.

'Well, he is bringing guests with him. And you must look your best to meet them,' Lady Symons added and Alys's heart beat faster.

It was a dull life at Throxton Court with her father away. When he was at home, there was feasting, games to play, dancing and news of the Court. Certainly there would be a stag hunt when he came home. It was springtime and culling the deer was a sport. She loved to ride but, being tender-hearted, was not keen on seeing the noble beasts hunted. But she was looking forward to hearing news of the Court in London. It seemed a fairytale place but, whenever she said as much to her father, he pulled a wry face.

'It may seem so to you,' he said, 'but these are dangerous times.'

He did not enlighten her further. She was not sure what way he meant, but she assumed it was because there were spies at Court, Spanish and papists. She had heard they meant mischief, but she never expected she would meet any herself. She was glad they had a merciful queen on the throne now.

Since the death of Queen Mary in November 1558, Protestants had slept easy in their beds, and now they were the ones in favour at Court. Her grandparents had spent many quiet days at home in careful seclusion during Queen Mary's reign before her own father had been summoned finally in his early middle age by the new queen and had been awarded a most important post, as Chief Groom of the Queen's Bedchamber. It was an honour the family had not enjoyed since the time of old King Henry.

He said it was very hard work and up all the hours of the night but, to Alys, it sounded quite enchanting to be surrounded by such gorgeous ladies and gentlemen. Alys longed for London and excitement. Often she yearned to escape with her father to Queen Elizabeth's Court, although she dearly loved her home at Throxton and the beautiful countryside around it.

At almost seventeen, she was ready to spread her wings and fly, but the Throxton family was not in the highest order of aristocracy, which lessened her own chances of being summoned. There were many girls higher than she who would be thought of first. However, her father had promised her he would take her to see the sights of London.

'But when, Father? When will you take me?'

'When you are less of a tomboy, child, and more of a young lady,' he had teased gently.

Surely she was that now with her long, dark hair and dark-blue eyes. She looked at herself in the glass now as Abigail tut-tutted, still trying to fix the ruff in place.

'Who is Father bringing with him?' Alys asked.

Her mother sat down on the oak settle.

'Master Alexander Huston.'

Alys swallowed nervously and Lady Symons narrowed her eyes.

'And two other young men, I believe. Master Nicholas Merson and his older brother, Thomas. They are our distant neighbours and I understand that, presently, they have been in London on business. It seems that Thomas Merson had been travelling on the Continent for some six years and wished to see something of our great capital.'

Alys's face showed no sign of the jealousy she was feeling inside. Young men could do so much, whereas girls were forced to stay at home and wait patiently for things to happen.

'As their home at Merson Court is little less than fifteen miles or so away, Master Huston heard of their intended return and requested them to accompany him and your father on the ride home into Worcestershire. Four swords are better than one, for these are dangerous days on the road with footpads, traitors and

5

the like. Of course, your dear father has invited them to dinner out of courtesy. But we have never known the family very well and I hope the youths do not intend to stay too long. We do not even know if they are companionable young men.'

Alys wasn't taking a great deal of notice of her mother's prattling gossip about their neighbours at that point. She was thinking about the other men expected with her father. Her heart, which had been rising high, had plummeted suddenly. To see Alexander Huston again would be worse than suffering Lord Sedley.

He was a young man she had no desire to be with. He rarely smiled, always wore black and had no love of fashion. His conversation was extremely boring and although he wore expensive jewels on his chest, he still looked like a clergyman. He was not handsome either. This was something she would not have cared about so much, if only he made her laugh. But he seemed to have no desire to do so! His heart seemed entirely set upon matters of state. And this was the man to whom she was to be betrothed if her lady mother had her way.

He had a fine estate and wealth to match, the greatest catch in the county according to Lady Symons. And he had a place at Court. Her father said that the Queen's secretary, Lord Walsingham, made much of him, but there was something sinister about Alex, cruel even.

She thought about their last encounter in the Throxton rose garden, which was one of the finest in the county of Worcestershire. It was surrounded by neat, box hedges and was the loveliest place she knew. She had been sitting with Abigail, beside the sundial, doing some fine embroidery. The girls had been laughing at some nonsense and the afternoon sun had been warm on their bent heads. But, suddenly, a long shadow had fallen over Alys's fine linen work and she had looked up into grey, cold eyes. With a curt word, Master Huston had dismissed Abigail, who had hurried away thankfully. Although she had never said so, Alys knew her maid hated him as much as she did.

There was something cold and sly about Alex Huston. His lips felt freezing as they kissed her trembling hand. He was not wearing the bright colours Alys loved but, as usual, a restrained and elegant doublet of black velvet. She had pulled back her hand from his quickly.

'Good-day, Master Huston.'

She hoped he would notice the haughty look on her face, which was meant to tell him he was not welcome to her favourite spot.

'Good afternoon, Alys. You make a delightful picture amidst the roses. In fact, there is no blush on the rose's cheek which can compare with yours.'

Alys had no desire to be complimented by him. She was looking forward to the day when some laughing lad would woo her. She had a strong idea in her mind what he would be like. He would be dressed in bright colours and his doublet would be sewn with the finest seed pearls. He would wear a wonderful lace ruff like Lord Essex, who was the leader of fashion at Court. Her father had described all of this to her. Oh, yes, Alys had an image in her mind of a suitor for herself, who was not in the least like Alex.

She had lain in bed many nights trying to decide how she could convey this news to her father. Alys was sure he wished her to be happy. He would not want her to marry Alexander if she did not wish it. She would have to tell her mother, too, but that would be more difficult as Lady Symons' heart would not be melted by crying. Alys knew she must marry well to make her mother happy, too, but she prayed it would not be with Master Huston.

'Ow,' Alys cried, coming back to reality, as Abigail finished placing the ruff and caught her soft neck with a sharp pin.

As Abigail arranged her young mistress's velvet half-bonnet, hooped with pearls, upon her hair, Alys bit her lip. Would her mother try to force her into a wedding with Alexander? Alys decided she would appeal to her father if she did and beg his mercy. Thankfully, her mother did not mention Master Huston again, but rose from the settle suddenly and walked purposefully from the room. A few moments later she returned, holding a silver casket. Alys recognised it immediately. It always rested in a secret drawer of the small dressing-table in Lady Symons' bedchamber. Alys had been shown its hiding place several times as a child, but was never allowed to touch. She drew in her breath excitedly now as her mother unlocked the casket. Then, suddenly, before her dazzled eyes, the Throxton sapphires twinkled like stars. The necklace was the family's most prized possession and Alys had heard her mother say she, herself, had only worn it twice—at her own wedding and to celebrate Queen Bess's Coronation.

'The Throxton sapphires, Mother?'

Her puzzled look turned to joy as Lady Symons took the necklace carefully from the casket and placed it about Alys's white neck. The blue stones flashed and sparkled in the afternoon sun.

'Am I to wear the necklace? Tonight at the feast?'

She was happy and sad all at once.

'No, Alys, no, indeed. I want you only to see how it becomes you. How the sapphires match your eyes! You are grown up now, and more than ready to take a husband. The stones are worn by every Throxton bride, as you will wear them in your turn, for your husband.'

'Yes, Mother, thank you.'

Alys gasped at her reflection in the dim glass. She could hardly recognise herself underneath the finery. She looked a bride already. But at that moment, Alys decided she would rather die than marry Alexander. It was then she murmured a prayer under her breath, that fate would send someone else to share her life instead of him!

Throxton Court was a lovely place to be on a late spring evening. Its mellow red walls and black pitched beams made a pretty picture as they were reflected in the broad moat, which surrounded the manor house. There was no drawbridge but a narrow stone bridge, which led under an arch, ornamented with the Throxton arms, into a cobbled courtyard.

Inside and around that gracious space, the old walls of the house overhung crazily, their casement windows flashing diamonds of fire in the warmth of the setting sun. Alys looked down from the open window of her chamber as she waited for her father to come riding in.

She knew what her mother was about down below, ordering the housekeeper, the cook and the kitchen servants to stir themselves and make sure the feast was ready in time. It would be the kind of meal that was only enjoyed when the master came home. But there was always plenty to eat at Throxton. Alys had never known hunger as the kitchen garden and the surrounding lands and orchards bore food and fruit in abundance.

Her lordly father was a just man and had wanted nothing to do with pushing the poor off their own land like many of the fine gentlemen of the time. Indeed, he made provision for the peasants in the coldest of winters, even bringing them up to the Court when the ice was thick upon the pool and they could not draw water. Therefore, on his return from London, everyone found their best to wear and their tastiest morsels to eat and were ready to lay it out for him.

Alys knew the servants liked her, too, but that they feared Lady Symons' sharp tongue. Alys was not afraid of her mother, but her deepest feelings she saved always for her father. Yes, Alys loved him best and could not wait to see him. But the thought of Alexander Huston became even less pleasant as the afternoon wore on. However, her inquisitive fancy was tickled at the thought of the other young gentlemen. She had never visited the village of Merson, nor the Mersons' courtly home, but a friend of her mother's had said that the youngest son was a handsome fellow. Alys glanced in the glass again. Maybe she was vain, but she wanted to look her best for her father and for the Mersons.

When the dogs began to bark, she knew the party was approaching. She heard Monkton, their old steward, hurrying down the wooden stairs. Alys pinched her cheeks to make them redder and pursed her lips hard to make her mouth the colour of a Throxton rosebud. Then, smoothing her dark hair back under the cap, she tried not to hurry out of the room, rather to glide like a young lady. Her heart was beating very fast as she walked down the staircase. She would have loved to run but she was not a little girl any longer to be swung in the air by her father.

Soon she was at her mother's side. Lady Symons, looking regal in her new plum-coloured gown, was almost managing to smile. Together, mother and daughter, followed by their servants, stepped out into the courtyard, which blazed under the warmth of the evening sun. The music of horses' bits and bridles jingling in time with the drum beat of their hooves was getting even nearer. Alys's excitement was growing every minute. Soon her dear father, who understood her needs so well, would be with them again.

'Do not jig about, nor smile so, Alys,' Lady Symons commanded as the horses and their riders suddenly appeared under the arch and came clattering noisily into the yard, breaking the quiet peace of Throxton. She added warningly, 'Although your father deserves your warmest greeting, you must not simper like a common wench.'

'Mother, I can't help it,' Alys burst out. 'I'm so very happy to see him!'

Next moment, her fine manners forgotten

12

already, she was running towards the leader of the steaming horses, her arms stretched out in the direction of the grey-bearded man in the great, black riding cloak. At the sight of her welcoming arms, he hurriedly dismounted and, catching his daughter's slim body, whirled her off her feet and round and round. Then, putting her down breathless, he looked her over with evident satisfaction.

'Sweet Alys, you have quite grown up! I have missed you so!'

Next moment, Lord Harry Symons was hugging his precious daughter close to his chest, holding her captive in his powerful arms as if he would never let her go. And Alys had no time to see nor attend to anything else.

CHAPTER TWO

'Good day, Mistress Alys!' the thin voice said, breaking through her happiness, making all the fierceness of her joy drain from her body.

Immediately her father released her from his close embrace, Alys rearranged her dress slowly to give her time to look up and face Alexander Huston. He was still sitting on his horse and, mercifully, the glow from the evening sun low in the sky was blotting every detail of his pointed features out of her sight.

Neither could she see the faces of his two cloaked and hatted companions, who had reined in behind him and were calming their restive mounts. Although she was longing to meet them, the sight of Alexander had put her quite out of sorts. She curtsied briefly.

'And good day to you, Master Huston.'

Then she turned quickly again to her father, who put his arm about her shoulders and began to walk her in the direction of Lady Symons who had been watching their loving greeting closely but, unlike her daughter, had not deigned to come forward to greet her husband. In that second, Alys found her innermost voice asking why was her mother so cold towards him.

'Margaret! How do you fare?' Lord Symons greeted his wife courteously.

She inclined her head.

'I am well enough, my lord, and glad to see you home.'

He smiled briefly at this warmer than usual greeting, then his pale blue grey eyes were piercing down and holding his daughter's beautiful deep blue ones with his own.

'Is our daughter not a picture, Margaret?' he asked.

'Oh, aye,' her mother replied dryly.

'Come, Father, I have so much to tell you,' Alys urged, embarrassed, drawing him slightly in the direction of the house, where Monkton had assembled the rest of the servants. She was eager to ignore the unpleasant sight of Alexander dismounting enthusiastically and greeting her mother, who had a soft smile on her face now as she went gliding towards the young man. Then Alys felt her father's strong hand detaining her.

'My daughter, have you forgotten your manners? You have not yet been introduced to our other guests,' he chided.

Alys felt her face going red. It was childish to blush and she was angry with herself, but she had no wish to displease her father. She turned just as quickly again and allowed Lord Symons to lead her towards the other young men, who had now dismounted and, great cloaks flying off their shoulders, were escorting her mother across the cobbled courtyard. Suddenly, Alys found herself in the midst of

15

the trio.

The one standing close beside Alexander Huston was an arm's length taller than him, and even taller than Lord Symons himself. He was powerfully built, looking more like a soldier than a courtier and he was extremely handsome! Alys's eyes, suddenly full of interest, flicked quickly over his green embroidered jerkin, on to his fashionable velvet doublet in a fetching matching shade of green. She glimpsed quickly at his prettily-worked waistcoat from which protruded the top of his elegant, linen embroidered shirt. She was afraid she was going to blush again for, as she looked up into his eyes, they were wide, dark and full of open admiration.

'Master Nicholas Merson, at your service.'

The young man bent over her hand and kissed it. He straightened up then, holding her still in his gaze, and added, 'Allow me to present my elder brother, Tom.'

'Mistress Symons.'

The other young man bowed low over her hand, but he did not kiss it. When he looked up, he was dark-haired and dark-eyed like his brother, but his gaze held hers for only a trifle, then drifted away as if he had serious matters on his mind. His clothes were plainer than his brother's, but there was a dignity about the rich, dark brown of the velvet doublet, enlivened only by the white frill at the neck and wrists. Yet there was a softness about him and the dark colouring suited him much more than it did Alexander, who always looked hard and sinister in his black.

Tom Merson was tall, too, and well formed but his clothing did not exaggerate it. Alys noticed a faint sprinkling of grey in the wings of hair above his ears. She felt instinctively that this serious young man had seen some trouble in his time. However, although he seemed preoccupied, Alys had a feeling that he had noticed every tiny thing about her. Then, suddenly, he was smiling at her in a brotherly kind of way, not like most young men she knew whose ways and manners consistently challenged a girl to take notice of them.

Yes, his smile was sweet enough, but not as sweet as his brother's, she decided. The latter was one of the handsomest fellows she had ever had the good fortune to meet.

'Master Thomas, you and your brother are very welcome to Throxton!'

Alys smiled, meaning every word. It was so wonderful that she would not be alone and at the mercy of Alexander. She could sense Master Huston standing silent at her elbow, knew that his cold eyes were watching her every move. There was no doubt he had noticed her interest in Nicholas Merson, whose admiring eyes were still fixed on her face. She was very glad and felt not the slightest twinge of conscience. Soon,

17

Alexander must understand she had no desire to be his wife, that only a lively, handsome, young man like Nicholas Merson could have any chance with her.

'Young sirs!'

Her mother's voice broke into Alys's thoughts.

'I don't know what Alys is thinking of, distracting you so. Into the house with you and refresh yourselves. Dinner is not far off ready.'

'Thank you, my lady,' Thomas Merson replied courteously.

It was only then that Alys noticed just how tired and mud-spattered all the men looked. Even Alex's cloak was streaked with dirt from the road. Immediately Alys was regretting her selfishness.

'Oh, Mother, I'm sorry,' she said.

'Nay, Margaret,' Lord Symons interposed, who had been watching the young folks' reaction to each other. 'Don't be hard on the little lady. My Alys has a soft heart and would not keep young gentlemen from bed and board.'

His eyes were twinkling, and to Alys's dismay, she felt herself blushing once more. To cover the confusion she was feeling and to avoid Alexander, she said hastily, 'Please follow me, sirs.'

They strode behind her, their feet hard on her heels. Alys was realising just how tired they must be. They had ridden a hundred miles from London and probably only stopped once or twice on the way. Her father had probably arranged for them to stay the night at his favourite tavern in Woodstock but the latter half of the journey through field and forest had doubtless been hard going and tiresome.

Once in the hall, Lady Symons called Abigail, who had been standing outside with the other servants and whose cheeks now resembled a bright red apple, to lead the trio of young men up the staircase and through the gallery to their respective bedchambers. Masters Nicholas and Thomas Merson were to room together, while Alexander had been given the fine, large chamber which overlooked the moat. Naturally, he was her mother's favourite—but not hers!

Alys and her parents watched the last flurry of their cloaks as they disappeared from sight above.

'Now, I must be off to superintend the kitchen,' Lady Symons snapped. 'You'd do well, my lord, to divest yourself of your outer wear for dinner.'

Alys caught the glance from her father's mischievous eyes.

'Ordering me about already, Margaret? That makes me feel at home!'

Her father's irony was just in teasing. But Alys was relieved to see her mother's gown whisk off below stairs. It meant that she could spend some precious moments with her father.

Harry Symons smiled at Alys, then turned to old Monkton who had been standing behind him silently.

'Send John to my bedchamber, Monkton, to lay out my finery. Tonight, our feast is graced by some comely, young men and I would like to look as good as any of them.'

'You will, Father,' the adoring Alys added.

'Will I then, young woman?' her father teased. 'But you, my dear, will be the brightest star, a star that some young gentleman will pluck from the heavens one of these days. But not too soon, I hope.'

'Thank you, Father,' Alys replied, 'but I have no intention of anyone plucking me. You make me sound like a brown hen!'

Her father laughed out loud at her wit.

'Your mother may have something to say about that,' he added, suddenly serious.

'Yes, Father,' Alys replied determinedly, 'but I would like to say something about it, too.'

'Would you?' her father said. 'I sense dissatisfaction in the air.'

Alys knew this was no time to complain of her lot. He was tired and might not readily agree to her plan. She must bide her time for several days. Then she was going to make sure he was against her making a match with cold Master Alexander Huston.

'Not dissatisfaction, sir,' she replied lightly, 'but only caution.'

'What are you up to, Alys?' he said, setting his foot on the bottom stair.

'Just a girlish request, Father,' she replied. 'I'll put it to you soon.'

He rubbed his beard lightly.

'I see I am home now! And must be careful of my womenfolk.'

Alys put up her hand and stroked his face. She knew how to soothe and cajole when needed.

'Now,' she said, 'I must be off to my bedchamber to dress for dinner.'

A moment later, Alys was lifting her wide blue skirts and running lightly up the stairs before him.

An hour later, Alys was standing once again before the mirror being dressed by Abigail, who stood back and surveyed her work.

'Well, miss,' she said, 'you are beautiful. You will turn heads tonight.'

'Whose?'

Alys's eyes sparkled with fun. She did not have secrets from Abigail.

'Why, all the young gentlemen! But, miss, which one do you long for?'

'You are impudent, Abby.' Alys laughed. 'Any except ...'

She paused, glancing around lest any should hear her, but they were quite alone.

'Any except Master Huston!'

The girls giggled.

'Oh, miss, he's a sour fellow, that one.'

'Indeed he is! But what do you think of Master Merson?'

'Very sober,' Abigail replied.

'No, not the elder one in brown, but the young one, Master Nicholas.'

'Oh, miss, he's a very fine figure of a man. So tall and handsome. To be held by him would be beautiful indeed.'

Abby's dark eyes danced.

'Don't be impertinent, Abby! Do not speak of Master Merson that way.'

'No, miss, of course not!'

Abby pulled such a funny face that Alys was sorry for her harshness.

'I am a lady born, Abby, and must behave like one. But, still, I think, you are right. Master Nicholas would be a fair catch. Now, how do I look?'

'Wonderful, miss!'

The respectful tone in Abigail's voice told Alys she spoke truly.

'You may go now, Abby.'

The girl curtsied and withdrew. Alys walked over to the window, her gown rustling as she moved. It was dark now outside and the moon would soon be in the sky. She stood in the dim candlelight, thinking hard. She examined her conscience religiously as she had been taught.

There are other things to life than just a handsome face, land and lineage, Alys Symons, the little voice of her conscience nagged. What about a loving heart? Alexander

Huston had good lineage and land but, for certain, he had not the last. How wonderful it would be to find a young man who possessed them all. Perhaps Nicholas could be that man? What had her mother said about his family? Alys tried to remember now, what she had shut her ears to earlier on in the day.

'They are our distant neighbours and I understand that, presently, they have been in London on business.'

Perhaps her mother would not be against the Mersons. Business men made money. What business though? She had heard of merchants, but they were not true gentlemen surely, although Her Majesty encouraged her loyal subjects to undertake free enterprise and show bravery in doing so.

What about Sir Walter Raleigh? He did great business on the high seas. Her father had whispered to her that he was little more than a pirate, yet the queen was very fond of him. Nicholas didn't look like a merchant, nor a pirate either. She recalled his handsome features again with some pleasure.

As for his elder brother, Tom, presumably the heir, for all his sweetness of smile, she could not imagine him as a suitor. There was a great distance to him, which would keep any young woman at arm's length. No, it was Nicholas she liked. Alys's heart gave a delicious little flutter. Soon she and Nicholas would be seated at the great table, together maybe. And he would gaze into her face again. He did admire her, she was sure of that.

Her mischievous eyes sparkling, she arranged her voluminous skirts, pursed her lips to redden them and pinched her cheeks to give them colour. She could hear the sound of the musicians as they struck up below. If she did not hurry, her mother would be sending for her. As she stepped out of her room and paused on the polished black wooden floor outside her room, she decided right there and then that she did not intend to let her mother ever find out what she was planning until she, herself, was entirely ready.

However, Alys's plans did not go quite how she wished. Someone else had planned to wait until the last minute also to go down to dine.

'Good evening, Alys.'

She caught her breath as Alexander Huston came out of his bedchamber the very moment she was passing by it in the gallery.

'Master Huston,' she said and inclined her head haughtily.

Next moment, she was quivering as his hand was on her sleeve.

'May I tell you how well you look tonight?' he said.

'You may, but I do not enjoy it.'

She risked the answer. However, he did not seem to notice her rudeness, and his hand was still grasping her arm. He was dressed in that self-same black, exactly as she had seen him

24

earlier, but this outfit was not spattered with mud. The cloth was rich and heavy, but dour and sinister like him.

His face was close to hers and most unpleasantly so. Even to be near to him made her stomach quite turn over. She looked upwards at the portraits of her Throxton ancestors. They were no help, looking sternly down.

'Aye, Alys, they were the King's good men,' Alexander said, following her gaze. 'And, I assure you, would approve of our match.'

'What match?' Alys asked faintly.

'A match which is made in Heaven above,' he said. 'And which your lady mother wishes greatly. And your father, too.'

Alys swallowed at the words. He was so close he was creasing her skirt! She moved back and he followed, imprisoning her against the wall.

'Does my father know of this match?' Alys asked, trying to make light of what he was saying. 'For if he does, I know little of it.'

'And you are against it, Alys?'

'Aye,' she said, her eyes darting everywhere.

The little voice in her head was telling her that he had never been so near her, nor spoken so hotly before. It was a dangerous situation.

'But that is what all young women of fashion say when faced with an eager lover.'

'Master Huston, I have no knowledge of the

25

ways of love at Court,' Alys replied, thrusting out her chin. 'I am a girl bred into country ways. I wish to marry for love and not be constrained.'

He laughed aloud and bowed.

'Love, Alys, is what I speak of also. I am a country lad myself, and nothing would give me more pleasure than to enjoy the simple life with you. But, when we are wed, we shall take our pleasure at Court.'

'At Court?'

'Aye, Alys. You wish for the queen's notice, do you not? I am made much of by Lord Walsingham, who has the ear of the queen herself. He likes his men to be married. It keeps them chaste. He has it in mind for me to marry and raise sons. As I do!'

Alys was near to panic. Then she pulled herself together.

'Sir! Do not speak of marriage nor raising children!' she said hotly. 'I have no wish to hear, having no knowledge of such things.'

'But, Alys, you must!' Alexander replied suavely. 'That is why a man marries, to have a son and heir.'

His hands groped for hers and found them. She could not free them. Even though he was tall and thin, he had a strong grip, which pressed the rings on her fingers together and hurt her. She gasped in pain.

'I know my father has not consented to a match between us, otherwise he would have

26

told me.'

She was willing to try anything to get free.

'He will, and soon. I have everything to give you, Alys, land, money and a loving heart. By God, Alys, I feel some passion for you!'

It was the first time she had ever seen colour in his sallow cheeks. His face was near to hers. Suddenly, she was very much afraid.

'Let me go, sir! I will not allow such freedoms.'

Alys wrenched herself free. He toppled back in surprise as she began to run down the long gallery. She could hear the leather of his shoes creak after her. At that blessed moment, Abigail and Monkton appeared, coming from the opposite direction.

'Why, miss, whatever's the matter?' Abby asked.

'I'm late for dinner,' Alys panted, flashing a meaningful look at her maid, as Alex Huston gained on the trio.

'Come, miss, I will walk with you. Your lovely dress is all creased.'

She smoothed it down, and with Monkton close behind, Alys walked down the grand staircase and across towards the hall, which was the heart of the house. She knew Huston was near behind, but her fear was receding. He could not harm her with Abby and Monkton beside her. She paused to catch her breath.

'Courage, miss,' Abby whispered as she stood back. 'You are safe in company now.'

The table had never looked so solid, nor so welcoming. The silverware glinted in the candlelight and there was a great hustle and bustle coming from behind the carved screens which separated the hall from the kitchens. Her mother had had rush mats spread on the floors from which exuded the fragrance of herbs and there, at the head of the table, was her beloved father, who was rising from his seat, extending his arms to welcome her. She hurried across to him, hardly conscious of the guests rising from their seats, too, as she entered.

'Dearest Alys,' he said, 'you are looking very beautiful.'

'Thank you, Father.'

She knew her voice was trembling. It was then she caught sight of her mother's expression. Lady Symons' brow was furrowed with displeasure.

'You are late, Alys. I was about to send for you, but I see that you were suitably hindered by Master Huston.'

Alys shivered at the words as Huston came to stand beside her.

'Come, Alys, sit you here,' her father said.

Her heart leaped. She was to be on his right hand. She would have died if she had been next to Huston. But she was not! Could that be her father's doing? It was the eldest Merson she was seated by and opposite the other, and Master Huston was to sit close to her mother!

Alys felt gladness and revulsion all at once. She was saved again. But what would she do afterwards? She was a pawn in her mother's hands. All she could do was petition her father. But could he, too, have agreed to a match between her and that devil? She sat down, still trembling.

'Miss Alys,' Tom Merson said, sitting down, too, followed by the others, 'will you take some sugar in your wine. You look very pale.'

'Thank you, sir,' she said, purposely ignoring her mother's looks.

Alys was not allowed to drink wine, but she needed it to warm her cold bones. He was offering her the silver cup. She sipped the liquid gratefully and some warmth began to return to her body.

The eldest Merson had the kindest eyes. It was then she noticed he took no strong drink himself, only water from the pitcher. His look told her he understood she was hurt and afraid and she relaxed in that tender gaze. Until then, she had not dared to look at his brother, who was placed next to the hateful Alexander, in case the latter thought she was looking at him.

But Alys had always been a spirited girl and, already, the shock was beginning to wear off, to be replaced with a justifiable anger. How could Huston have taken such rude freedoms with her? She looked across haughtily, ignoring his sallow face. Then she directed her glance at Nicholas.

He was leaning forward across the table, staring at her, too. He was indeed a handsome young man. His expression was admiring, but kind.

'Miss Alys, may I say how wonderful you look tonight? You remind me of the goddess of spring, Persephone herself!'

His brother smiled at his words and his dark eyes twinkled. Alys was relaxing in their company. Suddenly, she was feeling safe again. Huston could not hurt her while she was with them and her father.

'Thank you, sir,' she replied and blushed.

Her spirits returned as John, her father's body servant, carried in a decorated dish, bearing the first course. As course followed course, the guests grew jolly. Soon her father was standing to propose a toast to Good Queen Bess to which the guests applauded roundly, then followed a toast to the guests themselves.

Finally, he turned towards Alys and announced, 'The next toast is to my lovely daughter, the queen of this feast!'

The men were on their feet again, raising their cups of wine.

'To Alys!'

Her name resounded throughout the hall merrily. She blushed again but then went cold with horror as Alexander Huston, his voice thick with drink, added loudly, 'Yes, to the lovely Alys Symons who, I hope, will make me the luckiest man alive!'

She saw her mother's slight pull at Huston's black sleeve and her father's quick glance at them both. But it was Nicholas's look she minded most. Did he think that she was already promised in marriage to Alexander Huston? She just could not bear the thought. She would die if he did!

CHAPTER THREE

Alys woke very early to the greenest of spring mornings. As she came to, her aching head flooded with memories of last night's feast and the events which had gone before. The fervent prayers she had uttered before she retired had done little to ease her mind, or her sleep.

Suddenly, Alys longed for her carefree childhood, when she used to rise from her cot at five before her mother was awake and go tiptoeing through the wet grass of the Throxton gardens to look for fairy rings. But now she was grown up and waking into sheer misery. She had had such frightful dreams which, suddenly, she was remembering vividly!

She shuddered involuntarily thinking of the dark mists of sleep that had plunged her night spirit into the rarest of nightmares. She had been a bride to Huston in her dreams, which was a monstrous thought. No young girl should dread her wedding day, nor her husband.

'Oh, no, please no,' she whispered into the warm goosedown of her pillow. 'I would rather remain unwed for life.'

Suddenly, Alys felt quite wearied. In her heart, she was deciding that she must remain in control of her destiny for as long as she could. It was inevitable she would marry someone some time and grace her husband's home and lands, but, never, never would her groom be Master Huston.

Alys reached for the heavy drapes of her four-poster bed. Stretching, she drew back the curtains. Dust blew from the red velvet hangings as she unsettled them, letting the friendly sun rush into her spacious bedroom and make the particles of dust dance crazily in the yellow shaft of light breaking against and through the casement windows.

She stood up and shook her dark curls free from under her night cap. It flowed in a burnished mass over the intricate shoulder stitching of her shift. She reached to ring the little bell beside her bed and summon her maid to come and dress her.

'You look very flushed, mistress,' the girl said as she came into the room carrying a pitcher and bowl. 'Are you well this morning?'

Suddenly, the girl's eyes danced with mischief.

'May hap it was Master Nicholas Merson who put such colour into your cheeks with his pretty words.'

Alys could not help but smile. It was good to have Abby sport with her. It seemed to drive her serious thoughts right out of her head.

'You have a common mind, Abby,' she retorted. 'How I look has nothing to do with what any young gentleman has said or done. Indeed, the heat in my cheeks has come from sleeping with my face in the goosedown.'

'A pretty story, young mistress, and one I hardly believe,' Abby whispered slyly. 'I know how it is when young masters are in the house and they are as sweet-faced and tempered as the two of them be over there!'

Abby winked and gestured in the direction of the corridor. She began to pour out the water into the large bowl and stood aside while Alys bathed. Abby then came over quickly and began to pat her back dry with cool little dabs. Then, leaving Alys, she went over to the long cupboard and began to lay out some clothes on the bed.

'What are you doing?' Alys asked as she saw the rich crimson riding habit come out and her tall hat with the osprey feathers.

'Why, putting out your riding clothes, mistress. There will be hunting today, or so Monkton says in the servants' hall,' she added quickly, not wanting to be seen to know more than her mistress, who was evidently not in the best of moods. 'Am I wrong in this?'

'When I have firm news of hunting, I will tell you,' Alys said, standing before her. 'Now, for goodness' sake, look out my saffron day dress with the daffy down dillies and the ribbons. It will cheer me with its yellow!'

It was one of her favourite colours. She had both day and evening gowns in saffron, the latter worn at the feast. She stood in her undergarments while Abby fetched out the dress obediently.

34

Alys smiled a little when she saw it, in spite of her poor spirits. It reminded her of all the nicest things at Throxton, like the greenest of grass, the wild flowers hiding under their leaves in the dell, the fresh, new smell of the woods at the bursting of the year. For sure, when she put it on, she felt like Queen of the May. It was then she remembered the toast they had drunk to her at the feast and the look in Master Nicholas Merson's eyes.

Alys made a lovely picture as she emerged from her bedroom into the corridor which led to the long gallery. Like the hall below, the large chamber was a meeting place for the whole family. She could hear male laughter in the distance and the noise of the household. Her pretty head and spirits lifted. Of course, there were other men in the house who would do her no harm, her father included. He must surely be a safeguard against Alexander's unwelcome attentions!

Alys decided she must take care to keep with a crowd, try to make sure she was never alone. The thought made her hurry past the bedroom in which she knew her enemy had been sleeping. She looked up at the portrait of her grandmother, painted in the time of Henry the Eighth, which seemed to be smiling sympathetically as Alys dashed by. Whatever Alexander had said, she was sure Grandma would not have approved of him. She remembered the old lady only slightly as she had been just a babe when Grandma Symons had fallen ill with a fever, which quickly killed her. But the memory of kind hands and snuggling into a warm, protective lap came fresh into Alys's mind.

However, her dour male ancestors were scowling still from the murky depths of their oily prisons. Some of the portraits were blackened with age and needed restoration, a task her father was always promising but never got round to. He was too busy with important matters at Court. The thought of that lively place lifted her spirits further. Maybe he would keep his old promise and take her? Then she could get away from her unwelcome suitor. She had heard Lord Walsingham was not based there permanently and, given that Alex was currently in his pay, he would certainly stay close to the Queen's minister.

Alys had told her father that she had a request for him. Hardly words to describe how desperate she felt at the thought she might have to marry Huston. Now there was another thing she needed to ask him—either to take her to Court or give her the chance of another bridegroom. If he loved her, he would agree.

If only Nicholas Merson asked for her hand in marriage, she could still be saved. It was a forlorn hope, but the thought had comfort in it. Alys knew the young man admired her a lot, but marrying him would be a different matter altogether. She had taken a great fancy to him and most surely could love him. She glanced at her reflection in the burnished metal of the mirror hanging outside the long gallery. Abby had said she was beautiful. She had aristocratic blood in her veins and intelligent conversation. Why shouldn't she be fortunate in the way of wedding happiness?

She breathed in deeply and slowed down to a dignified walk. Somehow, she had to get her father around to her way of thinking and cajole him into persuading her mother that Alexander Huston was not the right man for her.

There were only three men in the length of the gallery, which was misty from the smoke of a brand-new fire. Alys paused at the entrance. Lady Symons had hurried out a few moments ago to chastise the kitchen boy for stoking the fireplace with green wood, which was causing curls of white smoke to creep out under the chimney piece and smother the room.

Nicholas Merson was leaning against the wall, talking to Tom, obviously about serious matters which concerned them both greatly, but in a low tone, in case his host should hear. But Lord Symons was making the most of his time at home. He was laughing and joking as he rolled the ball and scattered six of the painted, wooden ninepins standing at the end of the gallery.

'Come on, my young lords, 'tis your turn. And make sure you do not beat me!' Lord

Symons cajoled.

Nicholas and Tom broke off their conversation and turned to the game. Next moment, Nicholas had sent all nine of the pins scattering wildly in the improvised bowling alley.

'Well done, Nicholas,' Tom said, clapping him on the shoulder, but his brother hardly felt the congratulation as his eyes were fixed upon Alys in her saffron dress, pausing at the door.

'Well done, indeed,' she said, coming up to the trio, glad there was no sign of Huston. 'I would not like my head broken like those poor pins.'

'Yours is far too lovely for that,' Nicholas replied, unable to take his eyes off her beauty and feeling unwarranted jealousy as her father put his arms round his daughter and kissed her on both cheeks.

'She is a picture, is she not?' he said. 'By God, Alys, you have grown into a beautiful, young woman. I have not seen your like even at Court, except for Her Majesty, of course.'

'Thank you, Father,' Alys replied, seating herself at the embroidery frame which she kept next to the window, so the light would help her stitching.

Her cheeks felt hot and her heart was pounding. She had seen the look in Nicholas's dark eyes and it made her tremble. The young men came and stood beside her.

' "Keep a guard over thy lips and tongue,

and keep thyself out of trouble,"' Tom read, carefully examining the stitches, while his brother also bent over to look at the canvas.

But Alys knew Nicholas's mind was not upon her work.

'Have you finished with the ninepins?' she asked lightly as her father called for beer and cider to be brought in.

'I trust my game has only just begun,' Nicholas said softly, glancing mischievously at Alys.

'You are too forward, brother.' Tom smiled. 'Take care! If Miss Alys takes notice of the Bible proverb she is working on, then you will be out on your ear.'

'Oh, no, sir,' Alys cried. 'It is lovely to have some pleasant conversation. I have been so lonely since Father went away. We have little company here at Throxton.'

'You have not been hunting nor dancing lately then?' Nicholas asked.

'No. We are secluded here, I'm afraid. I am sure you can't imagine how different Worcestershire is from London, Master Nicholas.'

'At Merson Court, we are not always merry either, Alys,' Tom said. 'But in fact, there is much to be said for a peaceful country life.'

'Shame on you, sir, at your age,' her father joked, watching Monkton bring in the drink. 'But I will soon put you to rights. At eleven, we ride out to find ourselves some venison.'

'And that will be good sport!' a reedy voice said.

Alys recognised it immediately. Alex had entered. He was dressed in the usual black, but he was twisting his face into a smile.

'There is nothing like a good day's hunting to make a man's blood hot in his veins.'

'Among other things,' Nicholas murmured, who was very close to Alys.

For a moment, she thought no-one had heard the remark, but a quick glance revealed Alex's eyes fixed on Nicholas. She could see jealousy flaming there and her spirits sank quickly.

'And will you hunt with us, mistress?' Nicholas asked.

'May I, Father?' she asked.

'I could not do without you, daughter,' he replied, 'and, by the look on these lads' faces, they could not either.'

'My lord,' Lady Symons snapped, who had come in unobserved, 'I need Alys with me this morning to supervise the house. And hunting is unseemly for a lady.'

'Oh, Mother, please?' Alys cried. 'I have not been hunting since Father went away!'

Her mother's face was set.

'Nay, my lady, let her come hunting,' Alexander Huston said, stepping forward. 'She shall be my very special charge, and no harm will come to her. I promise you.'

His bleak eyes glinted, and her mother's

face changed immediately. She smiled into his face in a satisfied way and exchanged glances with him.

But her father had caught Alys's sad glance and his eyes twinkled.

'Well said, Huston, but knowing your love of the kill, I think Master Thomas Merson would be my daughter's best guardian,' he announced.

Alys's heart lifted, then plummeted as Tom replied.

'Pray excuse me, my lord, neither hunting, nor killing has ever been to my particular taste. I would prefer to stay behind and read.'

Alys saw the look of horror on her mother's face and the sly expression on Alex Huston's.

'What? Read instead of hunt?' Lady Symons asked with a sneer.

'Aye, my brother is a true-born scholar,' Nicholas defended.

'And you, sir? Have you such scruples?' Lord Symons asked, his eyes sparkling again.

'No, my lord, I love the chase,' he replied, looking down at Alys. 'Have no fear for your daughter, my lady. I shall be at her elbow, too.'

'Then so be it, Margaret,' Lord Symons ordered. 'Huston and young Merson will take care of Alys. What more protection could she need?'

'Very well, my lord, but make sure she is not witness to the kill.'

'Very well, my dearest,' Lord Symons

responded sarcastically. 'Now, Alys, hasten away and find yourself a riding habit.'

'I will, Father, and thank you,' Alys cried with alacrity.

With four pairs of admiring eyes fixed upon her as well as her mother's disapproving glance at such eagerness, she curtsied before making a calm exit. But inside, Alys's heart was almost bursting with excitement.

CHAPTER FOUR

The crimson riding habit which Abby had laid out once more certainly saw some action that morning. Once or twice, when Alys jumped a fallen tree or narrow stream, she almost lost the elegant hat with the osprey's feather. She, like her father and the rest of the party, rode hard in pursuit of a noble stag all day. She loved riding and to be beside Nicholas was joy indeed. She did her best to ignore Alex. But she could not help but wonder at how inquisitive he had become.

Whenever they reined in, he kept asking young Merson this question and that, particularly about Tom's travels and business in France and especially both the brothers' ambitions for the future. In fact, his questioning went almost beyond good manners. Alys put his behaviour down to pure jealousy. Naturally, he felt that Nicholas was paying her too much attention and it was very clear the two young men did not like each other at all.

'Come nearer, Alys,' Huston said, as he pulled his horse's head round, reaching for hers. 'We have almost cornered the stag.'

'No, thank you,' she said coldly. 'I have not your taste for blood!'

But he was grabbing at her bridle.

'Let go!' she exclaimed.

'And I say let go, too!'

Nicholas stretched and caught the other side of the bridle.

'Did you not hear her lady mother forbid her to go near the stag? Let go!'

The men bristled at each other. Suddenly, Alys lost patience.

'Whether forbidden or not, I choose to stay here!' she retorted. 'Both of you let me go. I'm no bone to be picked over.'

They stared at her in surprise, then at each other heatedly, and suddenly did as she asked. Alys turned her mount's head away and went to stand in the shelter of a huge oak tree, where she could not see what was happening. It was then they heard Lord Symons bellowing.

'Here, sirs! Leave your charge for a moment and get you down here!'

Alex wrenched his horse's head round immediately.

'Come on, Merson, we are needed below!'

He galloped off without another word, but Nicholas stayed with her. Alys looked at him anxiously. Would he defy her father? She hoped he might, as she yearned for a few moments alone with him. He smiled.

'Don't fret, Miss Alys. Huston will enjoy the spectacle.'

'And you don't?'

'I can stand it, but I have much better company here.'

She blushed at his bold words. This time, when his hand was on her bridle, she let it stay. His nearness made her senses reel.

'Master Merson, you will make my father very angry if you disobey him and miss the end of the hunt,' she said loudly, to mask her confusion.

'Nay, your father is a tolerant man, and I am no man's servant anyway. He knows I will eat his venison with gusto even if I will not slaughter it.'

Then came the sound of wild cheering, accompanied by frantic barking. Alys knew the beast was dead.

'Your lovely face is pale,' Nicholas said. 'Do not distress yourself, Alys.'

Her eyes were suddenly full of tears.

'It becomes a woman to be soft-hearted,' he whispered in her ear. 'There is too little sentiment these days.'

'Do you speak from experience?' Alys responded. 'Are the ladies so hard-hearted at Court?'

'Hard-hearted indeed. So much so, that I do not wish to find one there.'

Her heart jumped. He must be trying to tell her there was no maiden in his life but her! They gazed into each other's eyes.

'You know, Alys, my lady mother feels the same as you about killing the deer. If she had her way, they would be free to wander all over our estate without fear. She has a kind heart and a sweet nature.'

'I should very much like to meet her.'

The words came out before she could help herself.

'Then you shall. When I return home, I will ask her to invite you to spend some time with us. Merson is a lovely house. It has a moat like Throxton, but it is smaller. There is a dovecote and we have many sweet birds nesting.'

Alys could have listened to Nicholas talking about his home for ever and she heard the sound of approaching hooves with increasing disappointment. Some moments later, Huston was back, his eyes shining unpleasantly.

'That was some hunt, Merson,' he said. 'Somehow, I thought you would have no stomach for the end.'

'Take care, Huston,' Nicholas replied. 'I am no coward and will show you so if you dare.'

He clapped his hand on his sword, and Alys was suddenly afraid. She had no desire to see the two of them challenge each other.

'No, Alex,' she said, using a softer tone towards him than she had ever done. 'It was I who begged Master Nicholas to keep me company. I was afraid. He was eager to go with you, but I reminded him that he told my mother he would stay at my elbow. It is I who have no stomach for the kill. I seem to remember you promised her the same thing.'

She could see that her well-chosen words had quelled the heat of a dangerous moment and thrown the hateful man off balance.

Turning to Nicholas, she added, 'Now, please take me over to my father. I wish to ride home beside him.'

Her quick-wittedness had worked, and obediently, the two rivals trotted along each side of her but, just before they reached Lord Symons, she and Nicholas exchanged a secret glance, which made her heart leap once more.

That night, her mother came to her chamber just as Alys was about to go to sleep, hoping to dream the sweetest things she could imagine. It had been a wonderful day, which had awakened her senses, but now Alys came full awake with a start. Lady Symons stood over the bed and looked down at her pretty daughter's puzzled face.

'What is the matter, Mother?'

'Well may you ask that, Miss Innocence!'

Lady Symons' face was set and hard.

'I have more than a notion that you care far more for Master Merson than you do for the man whom your father and I have chosen for you. I tell you it cannot be!'

'Why? What has Nicholas told you?' Alys asked.

'Nicholas now, is it?'

Her mother dug her fingers into Alys's tender shoulders.

'Master Merson has had the effrontery to seek out your father this night and inform him there will be an invitation for you soon to visit

47

Merson Court.'

'Yes, he said he would!'

Alys was ready to brazen it out.

'Did he? Then things have gone further than I thought.'

Her mother's eyes flashed fire, searching her daughter's face cruelly, making Alys feel guilty although there was nothing to be guilty about.

'Things have gone nowhere, mother.'

Alys was determined to stand up to her.

'He was telling me about his house and the dovecote there. That is all, I swear it! You can ask Alexander Huston. He was with me all day!'

'Aye, Master Huston has told me about the day's sporting,' her mother replied nastily.

Alex was a sneak as well as a liar. He had not seen anything pass between her and Nicholas. It was just jealousy on his part. He was trying to blacken Nicholas's name. Alys had a very uncomfortable feeling when she thought of the closeness there had been between them, how he had whispered sweet words in her ear. What would her mother say if she knew that? But how could she? Alys shivered in spite of herself.

'Please, Mother. Listen to me. I don't want to marry yet. I'm not ready! That's all I am thinking of.'

Tears filled Alys's eyes, not only from her mother's anger but from sheer frustration and the injustice of what had taken place.

'I must make you see sense. My mother drummed commonsense into me and I intend to do the same for you,' Lady Symons went on. 'Master Huston is the man for you. He is the one who will lead you to church, adorned by the Throxton sapphires. He will wed you, he who has more courage than some lily-livered man, who cannot stomach the death of a beast. He and that brother of his make a pretty pair. Do you hear?'

'Yes, Mother,' Alys sobbed.

She stuck the sheet in her mouth to stop herself from blubbering. She knew it did not soften her mother's heart towards her, but, inside, she was flaming with anger. She was determined to get to Merson Court somehow. And one thing she felt sure of was that Nicholas Merson's mother was not cold and heartless like her own, because when he spoke of her, his eyes shone with love!

Alys was not going to give in. She would make it her business to seek out her father the very next morning and tell him what her mother had planned. Alys never knew whether he realised how many tongue lashings she had received at her mother's hands. It was not right. And when she had his sympathy she would ask, nay, beg him either to take her away with him to Court or save her from Huston.

As her mother left her with only the

49

darkness for comfort, she imagined what it would be like to sleep safe in Master Nicholas's warm arms. The last thing she fixed on before she fell into a deep sleep, exhausted by the day's riding and the pain of her heartache, was that her dream of escape would become a reality and that never more would she be so cruelly manipulated.

The discovery Alys made the next morning saved the pain of speaking with her father. She had been walking slowly down the staircase into the hall, when she had caught the tail end of a most surprising conversation. She had paused on the oaken stairs, straining her ears to listen. She could hardly believe the words, which were floating like a gift towards her through the banisters.

'Aye, let her go, madam!'

'Then you are not offended, Alexander?'

'No! It will do your daughter good to see some new scenery and the Merson way of life. I have heard their home is a pleasant place and the family a good one. I would not stand in Miss Alys's way of visiting.'

Alys put a hand to her mouth in shock and pure delight. Huston was persuading her mother to let her accept the invitation to stay with Nicholas's parents! An inner sense told her there must be some reason for it, but she was so happy she did not need the warning voice inside her asking why.

'Then, Master Huston, I shall advise her

father to let her go. Maybe it will make my daughter more kindly disposed towards you.'

'I truly hope so. Besides, the young Mersons are presently in favour with Her Majesty and such a sop to the family may further my career with Lord Walsingham.'

Then the two walked slowly off in the direction of the garden door, much to Alys's relief, because she had even been steeling herself to speak to her mother after last night's confrontation. She knew, however, that the two of them would have to return from the garden at some time.

But nothing could make Alys unhappy that blessed day, even when it was her turn to stand in the courtyard to say farewell to Tom and Nicholas Merson. The brothers had already bid a polite goodbye to her parents. Tom, looking even more serious than usual, was already seated on his horse, when Alys paused by his stirrup. He leaned down.

'Thank you, little mistress Alys, for your hospitality. Soon we shall return it. May God bless and keep you.'

'Thank you, dear Thomas,' she said.

Nicholas had not yet mounted. However, her mother's eyes were fixed hard upon the two of them, as were Alexander Huston's. Alys gasped a little as Nicholas took her hand and brought it up to his lips.

'Goodbye, Master Nicholas, and thank you,' she said.

In spite of herself, her eyes were filling with tears.

'And thank you, too,' he said softly. 'This has been the most pleasant journey break I have ever taken, for it has brought us together. Adieu, my sweet, but not goodbye. Soon we shall have you to ourselves at Merson.'

At that, he swung himself into the saddle, his dark eyes shining. Alys drew back as the brothers rode out under the arch. She was determined to stand there until she could see their dear figures no more.

She turned at the touch on her shoulder. It was her father.

'Cheer yourself, dearest,' he said. 'It will not be long before I, too, have a tear in my eye, when I lend my daughter to the protection of those two young men.'

'Don't worry, Father, they'll take good care of me,' she replied.

Thrusting out her chin, she walked past her mother and Alexander Huston. Surprisingly both kept their counsel, having nothing evil to say about either of the Merson brothers. At that moment, Alys was too concerned with her own impending escape to ask herself what the reason for their submissiveness could be. All she could pray for was the coming of that wondrous invitation.

The message from Lord and Lady Merson arrived within a week and soon Abby was packing Alys's clothes into three great chests, which were to be transported by pack ponies. No-one, not even Alexander Huston, could make Alys sad from then on. She was even civil to him when he visited although, afterwards, she was afraid her civility might have encouraged him.

But he did not force his suit. It seemed that he was willing to wait awhile. He is so foolish, Alys thought in her new-found freedom. As soon as I am at Merson, all thought of him will disappear clear from my head. For I know that Nicholas is kindly disposed towards me and, perhaps, just perhaps, he will ask for my hand in marriage. It was a giddy thought, but it sustained her through the week before her visit.

Huston's frequent calls at Throxton and all her mother's warnings as to her punishment should Alys refuse her favourite were disregarded in the business of preparation for Alys's month-long sojourn at Merson Court.

CHAPTER FIVE

Had Alys really been at Merson Court for two whole weeks? The time had passed so pleasantly she could hardly believe it. She looked round her comfortable chamber, at the pretty chair, a linen chest, which smelled of scented sandalwood; a cunningly-carved prayer desk and sumptuous blue curtains, embroidered with golden flowers, hanging about a great tester bed fit for the Queen herself! Nicholas's mother had done everything in her power to make Alys welcome.

Alys's soft neck had been relieved of cruel prickling, because even her ruffs felt unstarched when she had been wearing them, and she had happily discarded her tight corset for a white, linen daygown, which hung loosely off her shoulders. This morning, her hair hung about her shoulders in one glorious, riotous mass because she had not worn her night bonnet since she came to this happy place.

Every day, country plants and herbs were brought inside the rooms for perfume and decoration, while the cool dairy was full of wondrous things, like new-baked bread and cool buttermilk. And Nicholas had spoken the truth regarding his mother. Lady Mary was a sweetheart, who smiled a great deal and did not raise her voice, neither to her servants nor her husband.

That morning found Alys content to stay long in her bedchamber, where she had retreated after a leisurely breakfast. Since she had come to Merson, she had lain abed longer than she had ever done and returned to it often, which was never allowed by her mother. Here, there was no-one to make her do anything, therefore Alys wished to do much to please her lady hostess.

She had stood at Lady Mary's side daily and marked how she kept the house, something she would never have done with her own mother! She was learning housewifely arts and enjoying them. Besides, the servants went about their tasks with a good grace as if they liked hard work. Even the steward did not curse any of them.

Alys had brought Abby with her and the girl was becoming so used to the place as well. Alys knew that they had both changed and that both she and Abby would find it difficult to re-adjust to life at Throxton. But there were several happenings at Merson Court which puzzled Alys. She relaxed in the easy chair, padded with velvet, which she had placed by her window. Sitting there, just looking out, she suddenly found herself beginning to think about each mystery carefully.

First, there was Lady Mary's lineage. Both Tom and Nicholas had their mother's eyes most certainly. Hers were dark and full, too, almost Spanish in hue. But Lady Mary could not be Spanish, or her sons would not have been welcome at Court. Alys could hear clearly in her head the snatch of conversation between her mother and Huston, the talk on which she had eavesdropped when Huston had said the Merson lads were much in favour.

Then what Abby had told her, if it was true, could hardly make sense. But the girl said she had the knowledge from someone of good authority in the kitchen, that their hostess was the daughter of an Irish lord, whose lands had been restored by Lord Essex, the Queen's favourite, when he had sworn an oath of loyalty to Her Majesty.

Alys had never heard of any Irishman swearing loyalty to the Queen of England. But, sure enough, Lady Mary had a lilt in her voice, which did not come from any English shire. 'Still,' Alys said under her breath, ' 'tis no matter to me. Better to be Irish than Spanish! A lot better.'

Then there had been that meeting with Alexander Huston when she had journeyed first to Merson Court. It had frightened her greatly, and had put her quite out of sorts! She, Abby and her groom had had about two miles to go to the end of their journey when they had been accosted by some rough men-at-arms who looked likely to do them much mischief. They had challenged her right to be riding in the vicinity, saying they were on guard at Merson Court and that no stranger could approach. Then who should ride up alone but Master Alexander Huston, who bade the soldiers be off and worry Alys's party no more. They had obeyed immediately! Afterwards Alex was politeness itself, but would not explain what he was doing so far from home and how he came to be her saviour.

She had been afraid at first that the soldiers were hired to keep guard at the Court and, on account of their rough manners, she had begun immediately to wonder what place she was going to. But then Alex had assured her that they were just part of some troop which had been disbanded after the wars and that it was lucky he had been out visiting an acquaintance nearby and had come upon the incident by chance.

It was then that Nicholas and his father had arrived to meet and accompany her on the last stage of the journey. Alex had bid them all a courteous farewell and disappeared into the forest. Alys still did not understand why he had been near Merson, who those fellows were and whether her hated suitor had in fact been following her!

Alys could hardly believe Huston meeting her was pure coincidence, but Nicholas and Lord Merson did not seem put out by it. When she reached Merson there was not a rogue in

57

sight and she promptly forgot the unpleasant incident. But Tom had not been at home to greet her.

Thirdly and strangest still, Tom's absences continued as did his returns at dead of night. Six times in the fortnight, she had been wakened by the sound of horses outside. Each time, she had jumped from her bed and padded barefoot over to the window, just in time to see the flick of a horse's tail disappear into the dark or the flash of a sword in the moonlight.

She could hardly believe Tom's business ventures could be waged so late. Yet his unexplained and frequent absences at breakfast, or dinner, seemed to go quite unnoticed. And, several times, Nicholas had disappeared, too.

Alys lay back in her chair, telling herself she had no right to question their movements. She hoped against hope that the brothers were not out wenching. Surely not Tom, and could Nicholas be so untrue? Never!

Her heart beat faster at the thought of her love. The two of them had become close, but never improper. She could call Nicholas her love now; she knew she could. Every look between them, every touch of his hand, every soft word led her to the belief that, soon, he would ask for her hand in marriage. She was truly in love.

The thought of it made her senses reel. To

be wed to Nicholas Merson was her desire and it must be brought about. She would think and plan and think again, until it became almost a reality. It was up to her to take in every sight and sound of the place so that she had the right arrows to shoot into her mother's hard heart. The Mersons were wealthy and that alone must please Lady Symons. Such riches had probably come from Tom's business in European ports. But they were well-bred, too. Nicholas's father was a courtly, be-whiskered man with a strong character and polite words on his lips. He came from a long line of Worcestershire gentlemen aristocrats, whose ancestry was much like Alys's own.

Lord Merson favoured her, she could see that, and, after all, it was not his eldest son she yearned for, only the youngest. But there was a notion in Alys's mind which had planted itself there on its own. She was convinced that Thomas Merson would not wed. Why, she did not know, but there was something about him that was untouchable, a presence even. He was treated with distance and respect by his parents and all the household.

It was the younger Nicholas to whom his father turned in all things, and he had said as much to her.

'My Nicholas is very dear to me. I can deny him nothing. He will inherit greatly, Miss Alys!'

Strange words for a father with an elder son

in his home! But there was no enmity in the words. Strange indeed! Alys decided she would add these words as the fourth item in what she now referred to as the Merson mystery.

And now, once again, Nicholas and Tom were absent from the house, this time with their father. They had not attended the dinner table last night, nor had they come home with the moon, and not a single soul had spoken of it nor offered any explanation as to their whereabouts. Alys had asked at breakfast.

'Have the gentlemen gone hunting this morning, my lady?'

'No, Alys dear, they are visiting friends. They did not return last night, although they were expected,' Lady Mary had replied in her soft voice. 'Are you lonely, dear?'

'No, my lady, I am quite content but I miss . . .'

'Nicholas's company, I know.'

The sweet smile was lingering.

'He will be back soon to wait on you, I promise.'

But the men were not yet back and the sun was high. Suddenly weary of waiting for Nicholas to return, Alys decided she would ask Lady Mary if she minded her going out for a ride with Ned, the groom. Lady Mary agreed and Alys quickly prepared for the outing.

She had just got into her full stride on the ride when she was forced to pull up. She juddered to an ungainly halt as her mount's flying feet slithered on the grass. She had been galloping fast and was almost unseated.

'Hold, hold, stand still!'

The animal was very nervous and jerked her head up and down fiercely. The cause of her anxiety was a great branch which had near snapped off an oak in the wind and which had made the mare shy.

The violent pull on the reins had exposed Alys's white hand to the leather, her glove split right open. They were two or three fields away from the house, which could be seen in the distance. The groom, who had been following close behind, reined in beside her.

'What is wrong, young mistress?'

He caught hold of the mare's bridle and soothed the animal.

'That great branch, half broken off the oak to the right, was blowing in the wind. It scared her.'

She looked at her bare hand in dismay.

'Oh, Ned, would you return to the house and fetch me another pair of gloves?'

'Go back to the house?'

The groom was staring at her as if he did not understand.

'Aye, it will not take you long!'

'But where shall I find your gloves, mistress?'

'Find my maid, Abigail, and she will fetch them for you.'

'Will you be safe, mistress, when I am gone?' he asked.

'What a strange thing to ask. Of course, I will.'

Ned looked even more uncertain.

'I was told to stick fast to you, mistress.'

'By whom, pray?'

'By Master Nicholas. He was most explicit in his instructions. He said that if you should go riding, you must not go alone.'

'Oh, nonsense, Ned!'

The man looked shocked, and Alys continued, to allay his fears.

'Although I am most grateful to your master, I shall do my palm some greater harm than anyone will do my body in the few moments you are gone. Now, be off with you.'

He looked even more afraid! Evidently, Nicholas had given him strict instructions. Her heart warmed to her love. Then a tiny touch of petulance crept in. Nicholas evidently prized her safety greatly, yet still preferred to ride with his brother and father without her company. Alys was rarely given to malice or pettiness. However, just at that moment, she would rather have been with Nicholas than a groom who looked frightened to do her bidding.

'Go on, man,' she ordered. 'Nothing will go amiss! I shall wait for you over there. By the willow!'

'I will be swift.'

Next moment, Ned was galloping off but, as he went, he turned half in the saddle with that frightened look on his face again. When he was out of sight, she suddenly thought of the soldiers who had accosted her earlier that month. That was probably the reason Nicholas had told the groom not to leave her side. But who could hurt her here, in sight of Merson Court?

But, just in case, she walked the mare quietly into the shadow of the mighty willow, and looked idly over to the low, tithe barn in the distance, which marked the end of the parkland and the beginning of the hamlet of Merson. The willow's branches dipped close to the ground and it was pleasant, seated in the saddle, hidden by a cloak of branches.

Alys could hear the sound of the brook which ran behind the barn and she sat still, soothed by its tinkling magic. Then, suddenly, rougher sounds fell on her ears. Her mare became restive again, pricking up its ears. Alys's heart plummeted at the noise of galloping hooves. Not the soldiers surely! The mare must have caught her anxious pull at its mouth to quiet it, because it stood stock still as Alys craned her neck and saw, to her great surprise, a small party of horsemen making for the distant barn. As she recognised them with relief, a sixth sense warned her to stay still where she was.

Next moment, two of the group dismounted

in a flurry of cloaks and disappeared into the barn. Nicholas and Tom were the ones who had gone inside, while Lord Merson and three other gentlemen she did not know, were waiting impatiently outside. What was happening? What was going on inside the barn? Should she walk out and show herself? But, as soon as the thought had come into her head, Nicholas was emerging alone!

Why had he left his brother in there? And why were they all now leaving in such a hurry? She watched the group divide with a brief farewell and, next moment, Nicholas, leading Tom's horse, and his father beside him, were passing her hiding place and galloping back in the direction of the Court, while the others thundered away in the opposite direction.

When she was sure they were all out of earshot, Alys walked the bay mare out of the shade of the willow and towards the barn. What could be happening? It was then that the little voice inside started to tell her that maybe now one of the Merson mysteries could be revealed. Getting down from her saddle, she slipped the reins about the hitching post in front of the great barn door. The latch was closed and there was nothing but silence without and within. Alys swallowed, suddenly afraid.

What could Tom Merson be doing in there on his own? Was he in hiding, too? But from whom? There was no-one around. Anyway, why should this be? Her heart was sinking as she remembered what her own father had spoken once when he was depressed at the thought of leaving for London.

'Give me my house in Throxton with all its faults, rather than a den of conspiracy!'

He had been talking of how many unfortunates at Court had come to grief through idle words and secret deeds.

'The walls have ears,' he added.

Could this be conspiracy? But, no, the Mersons were all too good! Alys chided herself for her ungratefulness and, plucking up her courage, decided to enter the barn and find out for herself what had happened to Tom. It took all her strength to raise the great wooden bar, which latched the door and made the barn into a prison for anyone inside. The door creaked open as Alys walked through.

The great space inside was completely empty. There was no loft, just an enormous ceiling, arched like a great church, hanging with dust and spiders' webs. The floor was flagstones and there was no living soul inside! But she had seen him go in. She could not be mistaken.

'Tom,' she said out loud. 'Tom? Are you within? 'Tis Alys Symons!'

No reply. Alys was shivering suddenly. She put a hand to her mouth and coughed, then sneezed from the dust. There was plainly no-one inside. Then the familiar sound of a horse's hooves brought her out of her imaginings. Someone was coming. Perhaps Nicholas had come back for Tom. No, it was probably Ned with her gloves. Maybe he had some explanation. She heard the sound of creaking leather.

'Ned? Come in, Ned, quickly. I want to tell you something!'

She turned to the door.

'Come in, man! Don't stand outside. I want you to explain something!'

There was deathly quiet as a figure walked in through the door. It was not Ned! Alys stared in horror at the dark shape silhouetted in the sunlight streaming through the door. His frame was long and thin and he was dressed all in black! Alys almost screamed with shock.

'Good morrow, Mistress Alys!'

Huston's voice was cold as he strode over towards her.

'Why not tell me what you have seen, instead of Ned.'

Next moment, his icy eyes were searching her pale face.

CHAPTER SIX

Alys marked Huston's expression and the ugly look in his cold eyes. Gone was any sign of the tenderness he had shown to her previously. She had always believed this is what he was really like in private. Evil!

'What are you doing here?' she asked boldly.

'I am on the Queen's business, mistress,' he replied.

She stood silent, remembering all those questions he had asked about the Mersons' affairs the day they had been hunting the deer. Was it the same business then? She must take care.

'What did you want to tell Ned?' he pursued.

'Ned is my groom,' she said evasively.

'I know who he is,' he replied sharply.

'I sent him to fetch a new pair of gloves. These are torn. When I heard your horse, I thought he had come back and I was eager to tell him . . .'

Alys breathed in, hoping the lie would be believed.

'I wanted to tell him that my mount had almost thrown me again. It shied earlier on at a fallen branch.'

She was trying to calm herself, to give

herself the time to think.

'And that is a true answer to my question, Alys?' he asked sarcastically.

'Do you doubt my word? Anyway, how dare you question me, Master Huston!' she snapped. 'I am not some country wench you think you can master. What I tell to my groom is my affair and no-one else's.'

'And I say it is not,' he replied, his eyes swivelling round the barn.

Alys stood watching, her heart thumping. She knew instinctively that he was looking for someone else, and that someone must be Tom Merson. But where had his brother hidden him? In some secret chamber? She prayed that Alex had not crept up earlier and heard her call Tom's name.

'I think Lord Merson would have something to say about you ordering me about in such a manner!' Alys added bravely.

'Lord Merson? Were you expecting him?'

'No, of course not. I told you, I was waiting for my groom to return.'

She knew she had said the wrong thing. Had he anything against Lord Merson? He couldn't have, or her mother would not have allowed her to visit the Mersons in the first place.

'Is my lord at home?'

Alys nodded. After the shock of seeing him, her brain was working now. Whatever mystery there was at Merson Court, she had no desire to prattle any gossip she had heard to this hateful man.

'And Masters Nicholas and Tom? Are they at home, too?' he continued.

'I am not their keeper,' she replied. 'I dined with them.'

She did not add when.

'At breakfast?'

'Why are you asking me all this? I suggest you ask them!'

'Oh, I will, Alys, I will,' he said, standing very close to her now. 'Were they well at breakfast?' he sneered.

'I took breakfast in my chamber,' she replied glibly. 'I have no knowledge whether they were in the house then or not.'

Now his hand was on hers, exerting pressure.

'Unhand me, sir,' she said coldly.

'What were you really doing in this empty barn?' he asked, still holding her fast and drawing her towards the door.

'I told you, I came to look around,' she replied. 'It seemed interesting.'

'Interesting?'

They had reached the door. Alys gasped as he led her through into the sunlight. There were at least ten mounted soldiers waiting outside.

'Get you down, Perkins, and search the place thoroughly!' Alex barked.

As he addressed the soldier, Alys found herself shivering. The man was grinning at her.

She would have recognised his surly face anywhere. He was one of the rough fellows who had accosted them on the way to Merson!

Next moment, he and the others were leaping off their mounts and surging into the barn.

'Are they in your employ?'

'Not in mine, lady, but Lord Walsingham's!'

Her stomach turned right over. Walsingham was the Queen's spymaster. Everyone knew that. Her father had said so many times.

'Ah, I see that you have heard of my master, Alys.'

'Who has not?' she replied as lightly as she could. 'And I have heard, too, that he favours you.'

Alex glanced at her quickly and lifted an eyebrow.

'But what could you and Lord Walsingham be looking for in some village barn, full of spiders?'

'Maybe one and the same as you, Alys,' he said, grinning.

She could hear the men banging and tramping about inside.

'I don't know what you mean,' she replied, feeling herself go cold in spite of the warm sun on her face. 'I told you I just wanted to see what it was like inside. It is a very interesting place and quite, quite empty.'

The soldiers were coming out again, led by Perkins.

'Nothing, sir!' he snarled. 'We've searched well. The flagstones are firm and the walls solid!'

Alex looked as disappointed as his henchmen. The men swung up into their saddles and filed off quickly at Alex's command.

'Why, Alex,' she said, 'I didn't know you were so important.'

He was so vain he preened, unaware she was making sport of him.

'Now you do,' he said, 'and I shall be more so by and by, when I have accomplished my mission.'

He was unhitching her horse.

'Come, Alys, I will help you mount.'

She was so relieved to be questioned no more that she did not ask what his mission was as he helped her into the saddle. Then he leaned forward and took her bridle, twitching the reins out of her hand. She was his prisoner, not having the means to gallop off.

'Now we will talk,' he said.

'You, but not I,' she replied, thrusting out her chin. 'I have nought to say to you, Alexander Huston. And you can tell that to your master.'

'Aye, you have some spirit,' he said, 'but I have seen proud men and women brought down.'

'Do you threaten me?' she asked.

'Not threaten, Alys, warn. You would do

71

well to mind my words. Why do you think I encouraged your mother to let you come here?'

'I think nothing where you are concerned.'

But she had, and the question had tormented her.

'I trust you are the Queen's good subject, mistress,' he replied, 'and as I told you I am on the Queen's business.'

Alys nodded.

'Good, then listen well. I am here to investigate a conspiracy. It is an ugly word and there are men in this kingdom who use and practise it everyday. It is my job to sniff this evil out, and the scent has brought me here.'

'What scent?' she asked, knowing her voice trembled.

'Your gentle Nicholas and his brother, Thomas, madam,' Alex sneered.

'What mean you?' Alys cried, afraid for them and for herself.

'I mean that if you are the Queen's good subject you will set a guard on your tongue and your eyes, and watch, Alys, to see what they are up to.'

Now she realised that this was why he had advised her mother to let Alys visit Merson. He suspected that the family were traitors, involved in some plot against the Queen! There was no way she could believe it.

'You are shocked?' he added. 'I tell you, girl, that you will be well rewarded for your pains if you report back to me.'

'There are no traitors at Merson, sir,' she replied clearly. 'I can wager all who live there are the Queen's true subjects. Why, each night I have seen them drink her health and heard them speak well and passionately of England. I cannot play the spy for you on such kind people. They have spoken more kindness to me than I have heard at Throxton.'

'Should I report this to your mother then?' he asked slyly.

'Aye, if you wish, sir,' she cried. 'Mother does not care for me. She plans to give me to a man whom I abhor!'

His eyes flashed fire.

'Take care, Alys,' he said, 'lest I go cold on you.'

'You are cold already.'

'No, I am hot for you still,' he snarled. 'And, remember, Alys, who my master is and what he orders to be done is done!'

'Let me go!' she cried, tears stinging her eyes. 'You are vile, sir!'

Then her ears caught the sound of galloping hooves. She looked round wildly. It was not only Ned, but Nicholas, riding hard by his side.

'Thank goodness,' she gasped.

Next moment, Alex thrust the reins into her hands and with a false doff of his velvet cap, spurred his horse off in the direction the soldiers had taken. Alys sat shaking as Nicholas rode up, with Ned suddenly lagging behind.

'Has that monster done some evil to you, dearest?'

They dismounted and clung together.

'He can do me no harm as long as you love me!'

She was surprised at her own boldness. She felt him breathe deeply.

'What was he doing here?'

'I don't know. I hope he wasn't following me!'

It was all she could think of to say. Next moment, he was stroking her cheek with his hand. Then his warm lips were on hers and she was almost fainting with happiness in his arms.

When he had stopped kissing her, he said, 'Nor shall Huston or any other man ever do you harm, for I will protect you from them.'

'Will you, Nicholas?'

'Aye, that I will. I love you, Alys Symons, and I want to marry you.'

'Oh, Nicholas,' she said, her own heart almost stopping with joy.

Every rapid breath in her body silenced Alex's terrible accusations. Nicholas loved her! That was all that mattered in the world.

'And I love you,' she whispered before he kissed her again.

'Will you marry me, sweetheart?' he asked.

'I want nothing more.'

With her head nestled against him, Alys was sure that now he had declared his love for her, he would be able to tell her that the monstrous charges Alex levelled against him and his dear family were nothing but slanderous falsehood. She had to speak with him quickly about what Huston had said, but first she needed to know what had happened to Tom.

'Please take me back now,' she said, breaking away from his encircling arms. 'I need to speak with you, in private.'

He smiled lightly, but she could see anxiety in his dark eyes as they mounted their steeds.

'As you will, my love,' he replied, 'but after midday. My mother is impatiently waiting to feed us all, and I am very hungry. Let's go.'

CHAPTER SEVEN

Lady Merson had watched quietly as her younger son led Alys towards the end of the long gallery, out of earshot. But she smiled at them both as they passed, and resumed her fine sewing.

It had been two hours since Alys's encounter with Alexander Huston, but she and Nicholas had had no chance for a private talk. She felt like bursting inside when she thought of his proposal. She wanted to shout it to the world. But she had to keep her counsel, be guided by him.

When they had reached home, they had dined well. Alys noticed how very hungry Nicholas and Lord Merson were. It was plain they had not eaten for some time. The rabbit stew had been cunningly cooked, tasting of herbs and country cider, but the excellent food did not drive Alys's purpose from her mind, only made her keener to find the truth.

Alys sighed as they now found a quiet corner. She felt like she had taken all the world's labours on her own young shoulders. She must tread carefully in case Nicholas thought that she had a part in Alex Huston's spying. Alys could never believe that any of the Mersons would plot against the Queen. The idea was preposterous. But she had to speak to

Nicholas, at least, find out what he and the other gentlemen were up to and, above all, what had happened to Tom. But she intended to tell him nothing about Alex's intentions, nor what the latter had asked her to do.

'Come, Alys, you have a very long face. I have a feeling that this conversation may not be a happy one. Has your heart changed towards me?' he asked softly.

'I pray not,' she countered. 'Anyway, why do you say that, Nicholas?'

'I don't know, except I feel it here.'

He took her hand and placed it over his heart.

'Perhaps it is only because I am near the most beautiful girl in the world.'

She couldn't help blushing.

'Fie, Nicholas, your mother will see,' she replied, extricating her hand.

'My mother senses already how I feel about you and I wager nothing would give her more pleasure than you should accept my proposal.'

'I have already, dear Nicholas,' Alys replied quietly. 'But will your father and mother accept me? This is one of the reasons I need to speak with you.'

She looked down the gallery towards Lady Merson, whose head was bent close over her embroidery frame.

'Don't worry about Mother. She is a little deaf.'

'I'm not worrying about her hearing. I'm

only thinking that if my parents will not give permission, I may never see your mother nor any of you again.'

'Heaven forbid that should ever happen,' he said swiftly.

'Therefore, I have need to understand some things that I have noticed here at Merson,' Alys said. 'I must straighten out the things that puzzle me so I can return to Throxton with a glad heart and my defences strong.'

'Go on,' he replied. 'What things?'

'Why, just this morning, I was out with Ned, and, I expect you know this, I asked him to return to the house for my gloves.'

Nicholas nodded.

'I sat under the willow waiting.' She hesitated. 'Well, I saw you.'

The expression in his eyes reminded her of the day they had gone hunting together. Tender towards her, but fierce beneath.

'When did you see me, Alys?'

'I saw your father, some gentlemen, you and Tom. You dismounted and you and Tom went into the barn.'

She wasn't sure she dare go on.

'And why did you not make your presence known?'

'I was afraid.'

'Afraid? Of us?'

'Not quite afraid but fearful of breaking into some private meeting,' she said lamely. 'I thought you seemed in a hurry.'

'We were in a hurry,' Nicholas agreed calmly.

'After you went in the barn with Tom, only you came out!'

'Yes?'

'That's all.'

'And that has puzzled you?'

He looked relieved.

'Very much so. Why did you enter? Where did you leave him?'

The questions sounded so silly now.

'Am I on trial, Alys?'

She could see he was teasing and she wished she could have answered yes, truthfully, but she held her counsel.

'And that is all that worries you?' he went on.

'Yes.'

Just at that moment, John, Lord Merson's manservant, came in and whispered something to Lady Merson, who put her sewing aside, rose and left the room quickly. They watched the door close behind her.

'Well, as to the disappearance of my brother,' he continued, 'Tom did not disappear. He and I wished to check that the flour, which was stored in sacks for milling, had not been touched. After, he left by the other entrance and made for the village.'

'But you took his horse.'

'Oh, you sweet girl,' he said, taking both her hands. 'His horse was losing a shoe and he thought it best I should lead the beast home unladen. He decided to go on foot to Maycroft, the smith, and warn him to prepare some new shoes for his mount. Did you think he'd been spirited away? He went on foot across the field. Now are you satisfied?'

'Very well,' Alys replied, hoping her face did not belie her words.

Inside, the little voice was telling her that what had just issued from his lips was falsehood, which she had never expected to hear.

'And is the barn full of flour sacks then? 'Tis a very large place.'

'Full to the brim,' he said. 'Now, sweetheart, what other mystery do you wish to unravel?'

'None, Nicholas,' she said quietly.

He was lying to her. Had she not been inside the barn and seen for herself that it did not contain sacks of flour, nor did it have a door in the back! But, in spite of that nagging little voice of reason in her head, her stubborn heart was determined not to care. She loved this man. 'He had asked her to marry him and she had accepted. Her heart knew he was sincere. Nicholas could not be a traitor. There must be some other explanation.

'Good,' he said. 'I know you have been lonely, Alys, during my frequent absences, but Merson is a large estate and we men need to keep a wary eye upon it all. Just lately, matters at Court have been too pressing. They have

80

taken up so much of our time that both myself and my father have neglected our duties at home.'

'And Tom? What are his plans?'

'Oh, he is a law unto himself. We would like to see him back in Europe, making his fortune, but Tom will not have it.'

'What will I not have, Nicholas?' a quiet voice asked.

Alys caught her breath. Where had Tom come from so silently? There had been no sign of him in the hall at midday. He looked extremely tired and he was still wearing his riding clothes.

'My advice, brother, about returning to Europe.'

The two young men exchanged glances.

'Miss Alys,' Tom said and gave a low bow. 'Sky-blue suits you well. You put me in mind of a summer sky.'

'A pretty speech, Tom, but I reserve the right to compliment Miss Alys.'

The two were so jaunty with each other that Alys almost believed that neither had any cares.

'And, Nicholas, our lady mother would like you to wait on her in the hall. It is my turn to keep Miss Alys company. Perhaps we could take a walk in the garden. I would be glad of some air,' Tom added.

His eyes were bright and his cheeks flushed red. Then she noticed the mud on his shoes and cobwebby dust streaks on his hose.

Alys curtsied. Perhaps she would find out more of the tale from him and whether it would tally with Nicholas's story. It was then she realised with sinking heart that she was already doing Alex Huston's bidding. She was as good as spying on the man she had promised to marry!

They descended the twisting staircase with Tom in front. He turned several times to see if she was all right. Soon they were standing side by side in the outer courtyard, smiling at the antics of the ducks on the pond.

'How I love God's good air,' he said, breathing in deeply.

Then Alys turned from the ducks and suddenly noticed a man on the roof, working on the tiles. He was very high up, but his feet seemed agile enough.

'What is Ned doing up there?' she asked.

'He was apprenticed to a thatcher for some years and has a good head for heights. The attic roof has been leaking and Father sent him to check.'

'I wouldn't like to climb up there,' she said. 'Mind you, when I was a little girl, I often climbed down into the apple tree from my chamber window early in the morning, so that I could run through the dew barefooted. But that was a very long time ago. No dew walks for me now!'

'So old for your age,' he said, but he was not

making fun of her. 'And is that all you have to confess?' he asked, his gentle eyes probing her face.

She yearned to confide in him, but she was afraid.

'I fear I have done worse since,' she said softly.

'I doubt it, Miss Alys,' he replied. 'We all have our secrets.'

Her heart lurched. It was like he was reading her mind.

'But my brother has a secret no longer.'

'I don't understand,' she said.

'He has confided to me that he has asked you for your hand.'

'Yes, Tom, he has,' she said and blushed as she confirmed it.

'And you have accepted him?'

'With all my heart, but your parents and mine may have other ideas.'

'Fear not that my parents will be averse to the match when Nicholas confides in them. But yours?' He shrugged. 'As for you, Alys, you are quite sure? You have no fears?'

'None, except . . .'

She hesitated. Could it be possible that this serious, young man was involved in evil plotting against Queen and State? No, it did not bear thinking about. She did not finish the sentence because a fearful scream suddenly filled the air. They looked up in horror and saw Ned's body come bumping down the roof and land heavily on the stone below.

'Oh, Tom, he's fallen!' Alys cried, but Tom had already left her side and was sprinting across the courtyard towards Ned's prostrate form.

Alys hurried behind him, fearful of what she was going to see. There was no way any man could have survived such a fall on to the stone below. She saw John running out of the house and one of the maids hanging out of the window, a terrified look on her face. When she reached the spot, Tom was already kneeling beside Ned. He was feeling his neck and putting his ear to Ned's chest. Alys watched the dark blood oozing from the groom's head and spreading out on to the cobbles.

But, then, with a terrible shock, she saw Tom draw something from one of his pockets and kiss it reverently. With awe-struck eyes, she realised the object was a wooden cross, which he laid gently on the man's chest. Next moment, he was taking a phial from the self-same pocket and opening it. Putting his thumb into the oil it contained, Tom deftly drew a cross on Ned's forehead, then opened his shirt and made the same mark on his chest, on his hands, too, and, afterwards, on his bare feet.

Then drawing close to his face, Tom began to murmur. Alys's ears heard the unmistakable sound of the Latin tongue. Tom had anointed Ned! All the things she had learned in her childhood came rushing into her brain, tales of old Queen Mary's reign and the rituals her unwilling family had been forced to proclaim. Then she knew beyond doubt. Tom Merson was a Papist, not only in the pay of Rome, but a Papist priest!

Suddenly, she realised that John was looking at her keenly. The shock must be showing in her face. She looked down to Tom's praying form, up towards John, then back to the dark, red blood seeping over the stones. Alys staggered back into someone's arms. Next moment, her head was light and swimming. Unable to help herself, she fell into the darkness of a faint.

'I'm sorry,' she said miserably when she came to and found herself on a wooden settle, piled high with cushions.

She looked up into Nicholas's eyes. He was kneeling beside her.

'The blood made me faint. Ned? Is he dead?'

'Yes, I fear so, poor lad. We grieve for him. He was always a good servant, and a good man, too.'

Alys closed her eyes and held on to his hand tightly. It was all coming back to her—Tom beside the man's body, how he spoke the words over the groom. She had to say something.

'Nicholas, are we alone?'

'Aye, Alys. My mother and father have hurried to the village to break the news to

Ned's poor wife and parents.'

'And Tom? What is he doing?'

Nicholas did not answer.

'I know, Nicholas, I know,' she added.

'Know what?' he asked, looking at her keenly.

'Tom was praying for Ned's soul. I saw what he did. I heard the prayers.'

'What did you hear?'

Nicholas's voice was clear and even.

'The Latin words! I saw him putting oil on Ned's body, murmuring words over his body. Oh, Nicholas, is it true? Is Tom a Papist priest?'

Nicholas got up from his knees and strode across the dim room to the fireplace. Alys watched him with anxious eyes as he stood, staring into the fire, her heart begging for some other explanation. Then he turned and the rays of the dying sun flamed through the windows, framing him in fire, too.

'What can I tell you, Alys, but the truth? Yes, he is a priest. We are all Catholics.'

Alys gave a little cry, then put her hand to her mouth to stem the sound of her sobbing.

'Then you are dead men, all of you. When Alexander Huston finds out, he will have you killed.'

Next moment, Nicholas was by her side.

'We are told to love our enemies, but it is very hard to love Huston. His is a hated name within these walls. I knew full well what he was

86

up to when I saw him with you yesterday. Don't you think I know what he was asking you to do? I know why he let you come here. And will you betray us, Alys?'

She was terrified.

'He was ordering you to spy on us. Is that right, my dearest Alys?'

'How can you call me dearest when you know?'

'Because I love you and I am sure you love me. You are no spy, my darling, and we are not traitors.'

Alys clung to him and he smothered her face with kisses.

'I was so afraid when he asked me to spy on you. I wanted to tell you what Huston asked of me. Of course, I won't betray you. I questioned you about Tom because . . .'

'Because you wished to know the truth. I lied to you, sweetheart. I had to. I would have told you our secrets soon enough, before we were wed. But can that ever be now?'

'It will. It will, I promise you.'

'What? You still want me even though I am a Roman Catholic?'

His lips were smiling but his eyes were anxious.

'I was gambling when I asked you for your hand. I was thinking there would have been too much love between us for either to go back when, finally, I told you the truth. I was hoping against hope. It was wrong of me, but I

87

couldn't help myself.'

'I don't understand your religion, but I know you are good and true and would never plot against the Queen. That is what Huston accuses you of!'

'And you are right, little Alys,' he said. 'We wish Her Gracious Majesty no harm, in spite of the unjust punishment she deals out to our brothers and sisters of the Faith through the devilish ministry of Walsingham. Let me make you understand. The Mersons have remained staunch Catholics for many years, although they pretended otherwise. My forbears took the oath of loyalty to old King Henry but, secretly, they continued with their religion. Silently, they watched the destruction of our churches and abbeys and the murder of innocent monks, for Mersons were not the stuff of which martyrs are made. When they believed safer times had come, they watched again with horror all those terrible things Queen Mary did in her turn.

'My ancestors did not believe it was right that she should persecute poor Protestants either, for they are Christians, too. And now our good Queen Bess has turned the tables and tries to kill the Catholics in this country. She thinks they all love the King of Spain and would murder her in her bed. But she is wrong. At Merson, we love her but we love our faith as well. Do you understand now, Alys? We cannot give up our faith again. We have to keep it alive for our children. But it makes no difference as to how we serve our Queen. We only want to do both. I would give up my life for her as much as I would for my religion.'

Alys had never heard anyone speak so passionately.

'I think I understand, Nicholas,' she said, 'but Huston spoke of plots against the State.'

'Huston is a snake, Alys, like his master, Walsingham.'

Alys looked round in fear.

'Don't be afraid, my darling, this is not treason.'

'But he knows about Tom. They were looking for him.'

'Huston keeps a band of rough men, who are pledged to hunt out every Catholic priest and bring each one to justice. But that is not my word for such devil's work! He thinks he knows about Tom. He has been watching us for a long time but, so far, we have outwitted him.'

'But he will hunt you down,' Alys cried. 'I am afraid for you all.'

'You are afraid for us all?' he repeated gently, his anger abating. 'My poor, poor Alys, calm yourself.'

'But what will happen to Tom when they catch him?'

She rose to her feet and swayed unsteadily while Nicholas supported her.

'Why, they will kill him, Alys, but I do not

intend my brother shall meet a frightful death. I shall persuade him to return to where he was trained in France as a priest. But he had always intended to return to his dear England and keep the Faith alive.'

'But he must go back. He must!'

'But he will not!'

They swung round. It was Tom. His face was pale, but his eyes were lighted up like candles.

'She knows then?'

Nicholas nodded, and Tom looked down at Alys.

'Yes, Alys, once a priest, always a priest. I could not let poor Ned die without being anointed.'

'But how did you know I would not betray you?'

'Because you are good. I have seen it in your eyes, little sister.'

She didn't know how to reply, so she kept her counsel.

'Huston asked Alys to spy for him. He is really on to you now, Tom. You must return to France!'

Nicholas's tone was urgent, but Tom was shaking his head.

'I am not afraid. If I desert England now, my flock will suffer.'

He turned to Alys.

'I know you have wondered about my absences. I was out, bringing the sacraments to the faithful, and Nicholas insisted on coming, too, to look after me. But Nicholas is a hothead and will be caught one day. Sometimes, I think he likes living dangerously. And, now, I must get some sleep. I have not rested for two whole days.'

Taking Alys's hand, he brought it up to his lips.

'Let me kiss your hand, little sister. You have done a great deal for Nicholas already. He is too ready to die and now you have given him something to live for. God save you both. And now, good-night.'

They watched him walk from the room. Alys clung on to Nicholas.

'What are we going to do, Nicholas? I'm so afraid!'

'We are going to pray,' was his surprising reply. 'Alys, we have an important task to accomplish. I want you to meet me tonight in the long gallery at eleven o'clock when my parents and the servants are all in bed. Will you come, dearest?'

'I will, Nicholas,' she said and her heart was thudding madly.

'Good,' he said. 'And now you must rest.'

Later, the whole house was asleep as Alys hurried into the long gallery. She caught her breath as she saw Nicholas waiting as he had promised, standing by the great fireplace.

'My love,' he said, kissing her.

Then he lit a small sconce from the embers,

and beckoned towards one of the small, arched doors which were cut into the wall beside the fireplace. Taking a key from inside his doublet, Nicholas opened it and, stooping, led her through. They were standing in a small space with an oaken flight of narrow stairs leading upwards.

'Follow me,' he said.

All that could be heard were their steps on the well-worn stones. Soon, they were in a low, white chamber, bare except for two deep niches cut into the stone. There was a large, carved chair in the middle of the room and two massive ornamented chests. Placing the sconce in a bracket, Nicholas took Alys's hand.

'Sit down for a moment, please.'

She sat and watched him. Nicholas went over to the left-hand niche and, standing within, he pushed at the wall. Some lever was activated because it moved to reveal a dark space. Putting his head inside, he called softly.

'Have no fear. 'Tis I, Nicholas.'

Several moments later, he was helping Tom through.

'Have you slept at all, brother?'

'I have and well, although the space is small. Alys, my dear, has Nicholas told you why he has brought you here?'

She shook her head, dumbfounded at his appearance.

'Then will you, Nicholas, or shall I?'

'I will,' Nicholas said. 'Alys, my darling, this

is our secret chapel, our place of worship. This is where Tom says Mass every day he is here and where we all gather on Sunday. I have asked him a special favour. He is God's minister and, by this, I want you to be sure I am speaking the truth when I say I love you more than life itself and wish to marry you.'

He took her hand in his and his grasp was warm and tender. They watched as Tom lifted the lid of one great chest and took out a white stole, which he kissed and put about his neck.

'Aye, Alys,' Nicholas said, 'I wish that he could marry us, and he could, but we will save that for later.'

'Instead,' Tom added, 'my brother wishes to plight his troth to you.'

Alys and Nicholas stood before Tom and exchanged sweet vows of loyalty and love. It was all she ever wanted in the world and she knew he felt the same.

CHAPTER EIGHT

The following morning, Alys and Nicholas rode over to the barn, where so much had happened the day before. She had dreamed of him the whole night long and just the thought of them together was sustaining her.

As they rode joyfully through the fields, Nicholas told her how Tom had managed to outwit his pursuers for so long. It seemed that Merson Court had many places where a man could safely hide.

'You mean secret chambers like the one in the chapel?' she asked.

'Yes, so secret that even I don't know where they all are. But my parents do. When Ned fell from the roof, he was working on another one near the chimney. Ned was not only our groom but a clever carpenter as were his grandfather and his father. But Ned has a young son, who will soon be ready to carry on the tradition.'

They brought their horses to a halt under the very same willow that had shielded her and her horse the morning before.

'Now, Alys, I am going to show you what happened to Tom yesterday.'

'But will we be observed?' she asked, terrified.

'No, I have my own spies out. Huston and his pack of dogs are following another quarry today, another priest. It is whispered in our community that someone has betrayed him.'

'How terrible,' Alys cried with a shudder.

'Yes, that is why we only speak about things like this with those we trust implicitly. And that is another thing we have to talk about, sweetheart,' he went on. 'You know I did not want you to know any secrets because you, too, will be in danger. But after Huston's request and your untimely observance of Tom anointing Ned, I could not avoid it.'

'I? In danger?'

She had not thought about it before, but now she could see she was.

'Yes. You love me and, because of that, they will realise you know our secrets. That is why we must get away as soon as I gain your hand in marriage. If I do not, I will steal you away.'

She stared at him, puzzled.

'Away?'

'You asked me yesterday what we would do. Well, my darling, I will tell you. We must leave England.'

'Leave England? But 'tis our home! Where will we go?'

Tears started in her eyes. England was the only country she had ever known. She could hardly bear to think about leaving it.

'Hush, Alys,' he said, laying a finger on her lips. 'One day, when things are better for Catholics, we can return.'

'I want to accompany you with all my heart,

but Tom will not go. He said he wouldn't.'

Her voice sounded strange, as if it belonged to someone else. Alys knew she was deciding her fate, to go into exile, maybe for life, with no thought of anyone but Nicholas. That was how strong her love had stretched by now.

'I know, but I must make him. I cannot stand the thought of what he must face if he is discovered. I shall not escape it either if they take me.'

She shuddered as she clung to his arm.

'And they will hold you responsible, too, for not informing on us. I have been so selfish, leading you into this.'

'Not selfish, love. I could not live without you anyway. But I am guilty of no crime.'

'If you refused to give evidence against us, then they would put you to the torture. God forbid it should ever happen. That is why we cannot risk remaining in England. I am sorry that you have been put in such a desperate position. I did not wish to risk your life, too. At Court, I made sure that I gave my heart to no lady. But from the first time I saw you, I was lost.'

'Oh, Nicholas.'

She was terrified but, inside, her heart was beating madly because of his passionate words and because she was so loved. She remembered the vow she had made in her chamber at Throxton that she would rather die than be taken to bed by Alex Huston. Now she had found a suitor who cared for her as much as she cared for him. She could not lose him either.

'I love you,' she replied, 'and I will be guided by whatever you say.'

He jumped off his horse and helped her down, then tethered their mounts to the tree.

'I do not want to leave this lovely place,' he said, 'but I must, until quieter times. Neither do I wish that my parents or yours be put in danger. If I disappear to the Continent with Tom, my father will be able to convince his friends at Court we are travelling on business. Thankfully, he does have friends, but some enemies as well. At present, the friends are more powerful and have the ear of the Queen. She has always been generous to young men who seek their fortunes abroad and bring England a great name. But she is not keen on them marrying!'

He made a wry face.

'But there is no need for her to know. It can be a private matter if our parents agree. We have spun the story of Tom Merson, the merchant, most skilfully and, so far, it has worked, except with Walsingham and his pet toad, Huston. Alexander thought to trap us by sending you to us, but his plan misfired.'

'But my parents may not agree. My mother wants me to many Alex. As for my father, I do not truly know his mind,' she answered miserably.

'Then you must sound him out. And you must resist the advances of Huston. It will only be for a little while and then I will come to take you away whether they agree or not. You have never been very happy at Throxton, have you?'

'I have not,' Alys cried. 'I love my father, but my mother dislikes me somehow and bullies me in the hope I will submit to Alex Huston as a husband. My father knows nothing of it. He is away too often. But Nicholas, listen, there is hope. I have a certain way with my father. He loves me and I know he will try and do right by me. I am miserable much of the time. I am sure my father will not want me to marry a man I abhor!'

'My poor Alys,' Nicholas said tenderly. 'If only we could run away together now, without anyone knowing where we had gone.'

He had his arms about her and was looking into her eyes. Her heart thudded madly at his words.

'But I cannot. I have a responsibility to my parents, to Tom and to you. If we just disappeared, Huston would be after us directly and both our families would suffer. But if we play this game according to the rules, then we may win and cause little hurt doing it.'

They embraced, then walked over to the barn in silence. Nicholas raised the great bar and, together, they slipped inside. Nicholas led her over to a spot near the far wall. Then Alys watched as Nicholas walked quickly to the rear of the building and began to press his hands against the stone wall. It was then she heard a creak not far away from her feet and saw one of the flagstones move. Another hiding place!

Next moment, Nicholas was hurrying towards her. She moved forward timidly to meet him, her riding skirts picking up chaff and dust. As she approached, she saw the oblong flagstone had turned on its end and, suddenly, she was looking down into a narrow hole with a rough-hewn flight of steps disappearing into the darkness.

'Where does it go?' she gasped.

'Right up to the Court, across the fields and under the moat!'

His eyes glinted.

' 'Tis our very own secret passage and the way we Mersons have often left and entered. It was built a long time before Queen Bess came to the throne. But its existence is only known to the family and their heirs. And you will be one soon, my Alys. This is where Tom went, my love. He stayed in the passage for some hours, then when he thought it would be safe he made his way back to Merson. It is not easy to pass along. Crawling on one's knees for nigh on a mile is not pleasant for anyone. Now I must close it up again.'

Alys shivered as he did. The thought of poor Tom down there for hours really terrified her. It must be like a tomb inside. What was

99

more frightening was that Huston's men might have found the passage. She remembered how they had stamped their great boots on the floor. Next moment, Nicholas was coming over to take her in his arms again.

'Now you know all our secrets, sweetheart, and that's another reason we must get away. But not hastily, otherwise they will work it out. And I could not bear to lose you.'

'Nor I you,' she said, clinging to him.

'And, now,' he said, 'I am going to set out our plan. It is time for you to go home to Throxton.'

She couldn't bear the thought but Nicholas continued.

'Nay, Alys, we must plan carefully. You had come for a month and you have overstayed your time already. You may stay a few days longer in order to let Huston think you are playing his game. But, in reality, it will give my father time to prepare our cause. He is amassing as much of his fortune as he can so that when his sons leave England we will be well provided for. I am working on Tom all the time trying to persuade him, as are my parents. Like me, they fear for his life. The Mersons are known as merchants at Court and there is some truth in the tale. We really do have some ships lying at berth in Bristol and one is bound back shortly with a rich cargo from the Indies. But there is another favour I would ask of you, Alys.'

'What, dearest?'

'That we keep our love a secret just a little longer. Although Tom has all my confidence, I shall not tell my parents yet, only that they have nothing to fear from you, now you know we are Catholics. It will not be hard for them to believe. They look on you as a daughter already.'

'I would never hurt them,' she said. 'And, although it pains me, I will not speak of our love, although I would like to shout it from the rooftops.'

The next few days were taken up by preparation for Alys's return to Throxton and the dreaded morning had come when her stay was to end. The love in her heart for Nicholas had been hidden carefully as she had promised, although the simple ceremony they had gone through in the chapel was never far from her mind.

It was both sad and strange to see her gowns and jewels packed up again and to be dressed in the formal clothing she had learned to loathe. No more the loose sleeveless gown, but brocaded silk and hated ruff.

'I think you have grown, mistress, since you came here,' Abby said as she fitted the corset about Alys's waist.

The servant maid looked as miserable as Alys felt.

'Fie, Abby, I am as I ever was,' Alys replied, breathing in.

She knew it was not quite true because she had dined well.

'Your lady mother will not like it, mistress,' Abby warned.

Alys would have liked to reply she did not care but she was a much wiser girl now than when she had left Throxton. She had to keep her mother sweet from now on.

'Then I shall have to live on bread and water,' Alys replied equably.

When Abby had finished, Alys looked at herself and felt almost the same as the girl she had been over a month ago. But she knew she was not!

'Are you sad to leave here, Abby?' she asked.

'Yes and no, mistress.'

'What a strange answer, Abby. Don't you know your mind? For my part, I am most unhappy to leave. Merson has become like home to me!'

Abby's spirits rose, her old boldness coming back.

'And is Master Nicholas the main reason for it, mistress?'

Alys considered the answer very carefully.

'Part of it indeed. But there are many things here that I prize. The food, Lord Merson and my lady's company and, of course, the ease of the servants. Abby, you know that very well, don't you? It is very different from Throxton, is it not?'

102

Suddenly, Alys wanted to find out how much Abby knew.

'Aye, mistress, 'tis a surprising place,' Abby added guardedly.

'How surprising?'

'The servants take to their work so merrily and even like praying. Take the Sabbath for instance,' Abby said, and Alys froze at what might be coming.

'I saw no difference here from Throxton.'

'Did you not, mistress?'

'We said our prayers as usual.'

'We did, mistress. But not in the same place as the rest. Where were they when we were praying?'

'What do you mean, girl?'

'I mean that Merson servants say their prayers in a room at the top of the house. That room is locked to all save them and the family. Have you not wondered at it, mistress, when you were left alone at worship? But I have been inside.'

'You have?' Alys replied faintly.

' 'Tis a very strange room, mistress. Quite empty with a big clothes' chest and two settles. And a carved chair, mistress, set right in the middle, and there are two niches in the wall.'

'Niches?'

'Aye, and when John pushes one of the stones . . .'

'Stop!' Alys commanded. 'I wish to hear no more.'

103

Her heart was thudding wildly. There was no doubt that Abby knew the secret of Merson Court. She was a sharp girl, but was she a loyal one.

'Don't be afraid, mistress,' she whispered. 'I know that you and Master Nicholas are in love, and I would not harm you.'

'You don't know what you're saying.'

Alys showed her anger.

'Nay, don't chastise me, mistress. You may be my mistress but, I, too, have my life. And my lady teaches that all men and women are born equal.'

'Which lady?'

'Why, Lady Merson. She has taken me to her heart and her home also. And I have found love here as well as you.'

Alys could hardly believe her ears. She had been so wrapped up in Nicholas she had taken no account of her maid's doings.

'Yes, mistress, there is a lad in the kitchen. His name is Peter Tully and he and I are in love and he has asked me to be his true mistress. And now I am begging you. Lady Merson knows the way of it and she says I must receive your blessing! Oh, please, miss, let us stay here, you and I?'

To Alys's utter amazement, Abby, bursting into tears, threw herself on the ground and hugged Alys's knees. All Alys could do was stroke her dark hair until the girl was quiet.

'Come, Abby, dry your tears,' she said when

the sobs had ceased. 'If this lad, Peter, loves you and Lady Merson approves, then I do, too.'

'Oh, thank you, miss, thank you,' Abby cried.

'But, we cannot stay. We must go home, Abby. No, don't say anything. We will return, I promise you. But, Abby, you spoke of the room above. You must speak of it never again, nor of any Merson habit, or it will be the death of both of us! And Peter, and Master Nicholas. Do you understand?'

'Yes, mistress. Thank you.'

'Now, dry your eyes and be guided by me. I have a plan, but no-one must know of it, not even you, nor Peter. You may tell him I approve, and I will speak to Master Nicholas and his mother.'

Next moment, the girls embraced.

'You have always been my faithful servant, Abby, and God grant, you may remain so. Now, come on, let us make haste to get the clothes' chest empty. The sooner we make haste to Throxton, the sooner we may return to this blessed place.'

CHAPTER NINE

Leaving Merson Court was a painful moment for Alys, but leaving her love proved to be the most painful experience of all. Her heart was breaking as she said goodbye to the Mersons, fighting back the tears.

'Be sure that you return soon, dear Alys,' Lady Merson said. 'I love having you here and, what is more, I cannot do without you in the house. You have been a real daughter to me.'

'Aye, that you have,' Lord Merson added. 'And do not fret. It will not be long before you see my son again. I promise you.'

Nicholas was to ride some of the way with her. But it was Tom who came to stand beneath her stirrup when she was mounted. He was dressed in dark blue velvet and extended his hand upwards. She bent over to take it. 'Farewell,' he whispered. 'God bless you and bring you back soon.'

She could hardly see his face through her tears. Next moment, she and Abby, who was weeping also, led by Nicholas and followed by two of Lord Merson's men, rode out to brave the journey home.

They parted near to the river crossing at Worcester and the only thing that sustained Alys once she said farewell to Nicholas was the thought that, whatever her parents did or said,

Nicholas had promised to come and take her away. Although she did not wish to go into enforced exile, she knew she must be with the man to whom she had pledged her heart. She watched him ride into the distance until she could see his dear form no more.

Throxton Court looked just the same as it had ever done as, finally, tired and hungry, Alys rode into the courtyard. Her mother showed ill-temper because Alys had overstayed her time. The servants seemed more downtrodden than usual in Lady Symons' presence and Abby had scuttled away silently as soon as she dismounted.

Later on, during dinner, her mother questioned her about every minute detail regarding Merson housekeeping and manners. Her father could not stand it and rose from the table before the sweetmeats came, thus giving Alys no chance to speak to him. But she made up her mind to speak to her father immediately regarding Nicholas. That promise she had made to her love was fixed firmly in her mind.

Lying behind the curtains of her bed, she also vowed never to let Huston know anything of what had passed at Merson. She was ready to play the innocent come what may.

The following morning saw Alys descending the staircase quickly. She was ready to go in search of her father. She had watched Lord Symons walk across the courtyard in the direction of the stables. Alys was wearing her favourite yellow gown, which swished over the cobbles of the stable yard, picking up dust and chaff. A young lad was bent, examining her horse's feet. He looked up as Alys approached.

'Is my father inside?' she asked kindly.

'No, mistress, he is over there in the close garden.'

He pointed to the gate in the wall.

'Thank you,' she said, turning.

It was a sweet old garden, surrounded by high walls. She saw Lord Symons then, standing by the southernmost wall, against which apricots, plums and pears ripened in the summer. Now there was nought but blossom springing from the gnarled old trees.

Alys smiled in spite of her anxiety. Her father would have made a wonderful husbandman, tending the soil and watching the plants grow. He had a love of gardening, saying that it turned his head from wearisome Court matters. Evidently, he had some cares that day because he was examining the blossom very closely, lost in his thoughts. He must have heard her skirts rustling because he swung round quickly to face her.

'Why, 'tis you, Alys. I thought it must be Margaret.'

'No, Father, my mother is superintending the cook!'

Lord Symons made a wry face and both were silent for a moment, glad they were not in that unenviable position.

'This is a pleasure, Alys,' he said. 'It puts me in mind of when you came to find me when you were a little wench and I carried you high on my shoulder through the garden.'

'I remember pulling the fruit off as I went,' she said, 'and how I used to scream when you tossed me in the air.'

'To be told off roundly by your nurse!' He laughed. 'But what brings you here so early?'

'What brings you here, Father?' she countered.

'I was hunting for pests in the blossom,' he grunted.

She laughed then.

'And I have come to be just that,' she joked.

'Your company never wearies me, daughter,' he said, sitting down on the stone seat, which was protected by a flowery arbour in summer.

She joined him. They sat together, each lost in private thoughts.

'I have missed you, Alys,' he added, laying a hand on her sleeve.

'Father, I came to speak with you about something which is troubling me. You want me to be happy, don't you?'

'Are you not happy then?' he asked seriously.

'I wish to be but I cannot.'

The words were coming out in a rush.

'My mother wants to marry me to

Alexander Huston, and I abhor him. She says you desire the marriage, too. I would rather die than be his wife! Please, Father, do not make me have him!'

He did not reply. She knew with a woman's instinct that he would find it hard to go against his stern wife.

'Please, Father, listen to me. You would not want me to marry a man whom I hate. To be miserable for the rest of my days?'

She could see he was moved by her words. He shook his head slowly.

'No, I would not, Alys, but you cannot stay a maid for ever. Would that you could! You must marry well for Throxton's sake.'

'I know, but I do not want Huston. When I was at Merson, I was very happy. I . . . I . . . found someone whom I could love!'

There! She had said it. He was looking at her keenly.

'Someone?' he said quietly.

'More than someone, Father. 'Tis Nicholas, the younger son.'

She was puzzled. He looked almost relieved.

'Although Tom is the eldest son, Lord Merson favours Nicholas and will see that he is well endowed. I have watched how he helps his father on the estate.'

'And is his brother not jealous in this?'

'Oh, no, Father, they are good people. They love each other greatly. I know Nicholas loves me, too. There was no improper behaviour

110

between us, Father. My mother will accuse me, but I vow this is the truth. We have spent such happy times. Oh, Father, please try to make my mother understand!'

'Sh, child,' Lord Symons said. 'Do not speak so wildly. Have I forbidden you to speak of Nicholas Merson?'

'No, Father, but . . .'

'Then calm yourself.'

'But my mother has set her heart on Alexander Huston as my suitor!'

Alys put her hands up to her face and shook her head.

'I know she has, too!' he said. 'And, Alys, she will take it amiss if I cross her. But I am still master of Throxton.'

He stood up.

'Yes, Father, you are indeed! Then you will stand by me in this?'

'I cannot promise,' he said, 'but I see you are resolved to love Merson.'

'Oh, I am, Father, I am!' she cried.

'And the lad feels the same?'

'He does, and he wishes to ask you for my hand.'

'And his parents?'

'They like me, too, Father.'

He smiled.

'And who could not, daughter?'

'And you like Nicholas, too?' she beseeched.

He put out his hand and touched her cheek.

'I have heard nought spoken against him in

111

my circle. But he may have enemies at Court, like his brother.'

Could her father have guessed why? If so, there was no hope.

'What do you mean, Father?'

'I mean that when a young man finds favour with the Queen, there are always those who wish to cut him down.'

The words pierced Alys's heart like a sword.

'And is Nicholas a great favourite?'

'Not great but tolerably so. Let us say Her Majesty has not yet allowed him to be seated on her cushion.'

Lord Symons looked stern.

'I don't understand, Father.'

' 'Tis a good thing you do not. And I must speak of it no more. But Master Nicholas Merson has a handsome face and, if I have heard rightly, will, with his brother, come into quite a fortune. Our Queen may have other plans for him.'

Lord Symons could see his words had strong effect. Alys was very pale.

'But I may be worrying you unduly. So Nicholas Merson has stolen your heart, Alys. Many ladies may envy you of that, for they have been unlucky. I have never heard tell of him setting his cap at any lady.'

'Will you speak to Mother for me?' Alys begged.

'I will broach the subject to see how the land lies, daughter. That is all I can promise. And, before long, I intend to have some serious discourse with Master Merson.'

'Oh, thank you, Father, thank you!' Alys cried. 'That is all I ask.'

'Come then,' Lord Symons said, offering his arm to Alys as if she were the greatest lady. 'We will walk in the garden a little more.'

Alys's spirits rose. With her father on her side, surely her mother could not make her marry Alexander Huston.

*   *   *

'You have a visitor, daughter,' Lady Symons said, sweeping into the winter parlour where Alys was sitting looking through a book of the latest musical dances. Alys was extremely interested in how verses were put to music. She played the virginals just a little and, at that moment, was imagining herself and Nicholas gliding through a stately pavane at Court. She looked up eagerly to see who could be visiting. Perhaps it was Nicholas come already. But she was sorely disappointed.

'Good day, Master Huston,' she said in flat tones.

'I trust you are well after your long absence from Throxton.'

'Tolerably,' Alys replied, not even trying to rise from the chair.

'But her manners have not improved,' her mother scolded pointedly. 'Alys, put that book

113

away and talk to Master Huston. He has come all the way from Warwickshire to converse with you!'

'Very well, mother,' Alys replied icily, laying the book on the settle.

'Too much reading does a maid no good, I'm afraid, Alexander. Something else she learned at Merson,' her mother added scathingly.

'Nay, madam, 'tis good that a young woman should educate herself.'

Alex picked up the book and scowled.

'Dances! Do you like dancing, Alys?' he asked civilly.

'I have no experience of it,' she said, shuddering at the thought of dancing with him.

'Did they not dance at Merson then?' he asked.

She felt cold. Was this to be the interrogation she had been expecting?

'I saw no dancing there.'

'What are our neighbours' pleasures, daughter?' Lady Symons sneered.

'Very simple, Mother,' Alys retorted. 'They do many enjoyable things. They hunt and fish. They ride, play bowls and skittles and engage in pleasant conversation. In short, they are cultured people as befits the English gentry.'

'They have evidently made an impression on you.'

Lady Symons laid her hand on Alex Huston's sleeve.

114

'Now, you young people must have much to talk about. For my part, I will carry myself off to the kitchen and chide those idlers there into preparing good meat for our dinner.'

Next moment, Lady Symons had disappeared, leaving Alys alone with her would-be suitor. He drew up a chair for himself. Purposefully, he crossed his long, thin legs, encased in skin-tight silver hose. She fixed Nicholas's words into her brain—you must resist his advances.

'You know why I am here, Alys.'

His eyes were narrow, like those of a cunning fox.

'No, Master Huston.'

'Then let me refresh your memory. At our last meeting, I demanded your help. Do you remember?'

She nodded, her mouth too dry to speak. She turned her head away and gazed at the tapestry on the wall.

'I am sorry that you do not look happy to see me. You should, because you will be seeing much of me in the future.'

'I do not think so,' she replied.

'But I do,' he replied. 'And so does your lady mother. Perhaps you will be more civil when we are wed.'

She must remain cool and in possession of her wits.

'You do not disagree with that then? Good. Now, to business. What did you learn at

Merson?'

'Learn?'

'Of the family's habits.'

'Oh, I learned a great deal,' she said. 'I learned that these people are good and kind, that they treat their servants well and that they are loyal and true subjects of Her Majesty. I did not hear one word or suggestion that could go ill with them. In short, Master Huston, they are all angels.'

He was silent.

'Indeed, Mistress Alys. And Master Tom? Was he an angel, too? Was he near to God? Nearer than the others in this saintly household?'

'Why do you single him out? I saw nothing amiss in him. He is a fine and honest gentleman, who showed me nought but courtesy.'

Alys was trying to choose her words carefully in case he trapped her into admitting Tom was better than the rest. From this he might infer Nicholas's brother had a clerical calling.

'How often was he at home, Alys?'

'Very often.'

'What did you do together?' he persisted.

'I don't understand.'

'Did he sport with you, like his brother?'

'What do you mean?' she cried. 'No-one sported with me.'

'But you told your mother just then that you

116

played games. Did Tom play games with you?'

His devious tongue was like the point of a sword, twisting and turning.

'I will not answer such impertinent questions,' she said.

'Madam, we are speaking of treason,' he snarled.

'I know nothing of Master Thomas Merson,' she cried, 'only that he is kind and good.'

'Indeed, I have heard he is very kind to all, especially dying servants!'

'What?'

She almost gave herself away.

'Alys, Alys,' he said, getting up and towering over her. 'You know as well as I that Thomas Merson is not like other men.'

'I don't know anything,' she repeated, 'except he is a good man.'

'And a good Catholic?'

He put out his hand and held her shoulder in a vice-like grip. So Huston knew about their faith. She felt very cold, but she did not answer. If she spoke now she might trap herself into agreeing. She collected her thoughts.

'I don't understand you, Master Huston.'

Her shoulder was hurting. She winced.

'Come, Alys,' he said, removing his hand. 'You have been with them for five whole weeks and you have not noticed how they worship?'

'I have not,' she said quietly.

'Did they pray with you on Sunday?'

'Yes,' she lied.

'From our common book of prayer?'

'Yes.'

'Oh, Alys, Alys,' he repeated. 'Poor, poor Alys. We know that the Mersons are Roman Catholics.'

'We?' she asked, her voice coming from far off.

'Lord Walsingham and myself, and all the Court.'

'I cannot believe you,' she said, opening her eyes wide.

'And I have to believe you?' he countered. 'You ask me to believe you do not know and, so, I will put this another way. If I was to tell you that if you looked upon my suit for your hand as part payment for the truth, then what would you say?'

'I don't understand you,' she cried, her voice cracking.

'Come, Alys,' he said, leaning forward and taking her chin with his bony fingers. 'I told you I will have you and I am bargaining now. If I believe you, and do these Mersons no harm, will you come to me willingly?'

She shivered and tried to free her hand, but he was holding her fast.

'Such lovely eyes,' he said. 'They have enticed me by their witchery, as they enticed poor Nicholas.'

'He is not poor!' she cried, wrenching free. 'He is a gentleman and he would never threaten a maid for his own purposes.'

'My offer stands, Alys. Your hand, or the Merson brood is delivered up for the Queen's justice. Think on it. As my wife, you will have gold and a name. As his, you have nothing to look forward to but the rope and the knife.'

'I have no knowledge of anything you are speaking about,' Alys persisted bravely, 'and I would rather die than marry you.'

'Would you rather see your saints die, Alys?' he replied coldly. 'I say, think on their kind of martyrdom. For I am ready to have them when I wish. But, on the other hand, I am ready for you, too, your most obedient and loving servant.'

Then he was backing off, but all the pleasantry had gone from his lips.

'It is in your hands whether they suffer or not. I will leave you to muse on this matter. But be quick about it. God be with you until we meet again!'

With that, he strode out of the room. Alys collapsed in her chair, her head whirling. She made an attempt to think clearly.

If Alexander Huston had evidence the Mersons were practising Catholics and their son a priest, he would have had them arrested by now. She had no illusions about him. If she agreed to his bargain, then there would be no chance of ever running away with Nicholas, never mind marrying him. She knew instinctively that Huston would not keep his word.

No, she had to keep her wits about her, but play the innocent fool as well. She would defy her mother, too, for as long as she could. Only in that way would she give Nicholas the opportunity to rescue her from Huston's clutches and save himself and his family. Alys had to keep a clear brain! And, even if her very life was threatened, she intended to do just that.

CHAPTER TEN

But matters proved much worse than Alys could have imagined. As she lay on her bed, turning time and time again to ease her pain, she went over the events of the week which followed that interrogation by Alexander.

Her father had been as good as his word. He had discussed matters with Lady Symons. However, his boast that he was the master of Throxton had so far proved that mastery over the house and his daughter's fate was very much under his wife's control. Alys had given up hope now of her father's skills of persuasion.

Since then, Alys had not been visited by Lord Symons once. Worse still, three days ago, she had been made a prisoner in her own bedroom with her meals brought by either her dour mother or a pale-faced Abby, who scurried in and out, not uttering a word more than was necessary. It was plain that her maid had been frightened to death and conversation with the girl would certainly lead to her dismissal. Alys had no wish to see this befall Abby, so she kept her counsel.

That night, when the moonlight was streaming through the window panes, Alys thought longingly of the world outside. She was contemplating escape most seriously. She rose stiffly and made her way slowly to the window. She had climbed through and down the apple tree many times when she was a little girl, but would she be able to do so now? And where would she go? Her outdoor clothes and shoes had been taken away.

She looked down to the ground. It seemed a very long drop. Even if she succeeded in escaping under cover of moonlight, she faced very real risks alone on the open road from footpads, soldiers and villains. There would be sympathetic folk in the village but, if they concealed her and she was discovered, their penalty would be severe.

Yet, if she stayed a prisoner in her room, and defied her mother as she had done every day so far, she would probably die of chastisement. Her mother had resorted several times to beating her with a birch, and her body was bruised and sore. But Alys had proved more stubborn than she believed she could. She had screamed at her mother tonight, like every night for the last three days.

'However much you beat me, Mother, or ration my food, I will never marry Alexander Huston. I would rather die!'

'You'll feel different when you are crying out for food,' her mother repeated.

'Does my father know how wickedly you treat me?' she had gasped.

'Don't look for comfort there, girl. Once I had made my displeasure clear to my lord, he set off on his horse and neither he nor his body servant have been seen for two whole days. Like you, he will come to his senses. Alexander Huston is the best fish you will catch, my lady. Instead, you moon and pine for a book-learned popinjay!'

'Nicholas would make ten of that cold fish,' Alys retorted, exhausted.

'Mark me well!' her mother screeched. 'When you are hungry enough you will change your tune and accept Huston as your husband.'

'Never, never, never!' Alys cried.

Her mother had laughed cruelly at this and left the dry bread and bowl of water on the stool.

Indeed, Alys was very hungry and sore. If only she could get a message to Nicholas! She had done her best to resist Huston's advances. She had not spoken a word during his interrogation. In short, she was getting desperate. Someone or something must save her soon!

The thought of her father gone away in her hour of need made her feel so sad that, in spite of herself, the tears began to course freely down Alys's cheeks. To cheer herself, she thought for the thousandth time of her handsome love. She trusted he would save her. She remembered the warmth of his kiss and his strong arms around her. Then she thought of his kind and gentle brother; of his parents, Lord and Lady Merson; and even their happy servants. She pulled her mantle about her and cuddled into the window-seat, her nose pressed against one of the panes.

She must have fallen asleep there. Alys shivered with cold and wondered what had woken her so suddenly. As she tried to stir her body, she heard the tapping. Someone was knocking softly upon her door. Alys got up from the window-seat and hurried over as quickly as her stiff limbs would let her. Next moment, she heard the key grating in the lock.

'Who is it?' she whispered, knowing it could not be her mother at such an early hour.

' 'Tis your father, Alys.'

His low voice brought warmth into her freezing body. Next moment, he was inside her room and taking her in his arms. She buried her head in his shoulder and sobbed.

'Mother said you had gone and left me.'

'I would never leave you, daughter.'

He hugged her close and she cried out in pain.

'What ails you, Alys?'

'Oh, Father, she has beaten me, because I will not have Huston.'

She looked up into his eyes and the moonlight revealed his horror-struck look. Next moment, he released her and struck a flint, setting the taper alight. Holding up the candle, he advanced once more.

'What has she done to you, dearest?'

'No, Father, don't look. It is nothing.'

124

But he turned her and looked down the back of her shift.

'What has she done?' he repeated as if he could not believe his eyes.

Next moment, he set down the candle and, as if Alys was a feather, he picked her up and carried her over to the bed. He laid her on it gently as he had done many times when she was a small child.

'Lie easy, Alys. I never knew of this! I swear I never knew.'

His eyes were full of tears.

'Don't cry, Father, I can bear it. She has done it often enough. But,' she added, 'I cannot bear to marry Huston.'

'Nor will you, my princess.'

'Will I not?'

She looked at him with wondering eyes.

'No, Alys. I told her that I would not have my daughter marry a man she hated. But she was too mad with anger to listen. She would not change her mind. She ranted and raved and I saw no way out, short of murder. Alys, I did not run away these last two days. I went to Merson Court!'

Her heart leaped with joy.

'You went to Merson? Why? Was Nicholas safe? Were they well?'

She was desperate for news, to know they had not forgotten her.

'Aye, they were. Lord Merson and I had much discussion and together we resolved that you and young Nicholas be wed.'

'Oh, Father, Father!'

Alys clung to him.

'But how?'

'Although 'tis the way of the coward, I have come into my own house like a thief by night. You must understand something, Alys. Your mother was not always like this. She has suffered much pain and loss. She is unkind now but, once, she was not. I realise that the love I had for her and she for me has died. It died with our son, James, the little one you never knew, who was taken to God at one year old. Four dead boys in all! Too much for one mother to suffer. With each death she grew more bitter. Alys, I believe that when she looks at you, it is like a knife in her heart. She doted on James especially, he who lived longest. You, as sole survivor, are both him and her own self rolled into one. Most sadly, her love has transformed itself into pure ambition. But such evil!'

He shook his head.

'I swear I did not know how cruelly she used you. But, I promise, she will never do so again. Outside, beyond the village, your Nicholas and his body servant are waiting.'

Alys could hardly believe it.

'It is true, Alys. They accompanied me here and they are waiting for you by the river. I know it means I will lose you, too.'

He passed a hand over his forehead as if he

126

could not bear the thought.

'No, Father, you won't lose me. I will come back, I promise. I could leave you for ever no more than you could leave me. Oh, Father, thank you!' Alys cried, looking round the room. 'But how shall I go to him like this? I have no clothes.'

'I have woken your maid and she has found a riding habit and some other clothes for you. She is waiting downstairs. There is provision made for her, too. But can you ride in such a state?'

He touched her back tenderly.

'I would ride to meet Nicholas no matter what!'

She was struggling to her feet already.

'Well said, my brave daughter. Lean on me now,' Lord Symons replied, putting her mantle around her shoulders.

'But what will you do, Father, when she finds out I am gone?'

Alys was leaning against him gratefully. She found she was weak and dizzy, not only with hunger, but excitement.

'I shall dream up some fantastic story to tell her,' he said.

'And what about Huston?'

'Brave Nicholas has his measure. Now come. Dawn breaks soon.'

Together, they stole down the gallery like thieves in the night. At the foot of the staircase, a cloaked Abby was waiting. Lord

127

Symons kept watch as the girls withdrew into the hall and the maid helped Alys put on the riding habit. They hurried through the courtyard then under the arch. Outside, John was waiting on the grass, holding the restive horses. Soon, the four of them were riding out of Throxton, keeping off the cobbles to save the horses' hooves being heard.

Alys looked over her shoulder only once as she left Throxton Court. Then she was tossing the tears from eyes, tears, which came with the great hurt she was feeling both inside and out, but also tears of joy, from the knowledge that she was free at last.

CHAPTER ELEVEN

To be in Nicholas's arms again was joy. To look into his eyes and see love there, bright like the dawn, was pure peace. Alys felt no embarrassment showing such feelings in front of her father.

Lord Symons had let the lovers have a private meeting. He and the faithful John had withdrawn a little distance from them, while the servant, whom Nicholas had brought, had retired with the maid, Abigail, to the cover of a thicket nearby. The girl seemed to have been very pleased to see the lad, Peter, and greeted him most warmly. She must have known him from the servants' hall.

So many thoughts passed through Lord Symons' mind as he watched Nicholas Merson and his only daughter wrapped up in each other. He could scarce remember wooing Margaret, but he had tasted love's pleasures and would not deny them to Alys. He turned to John and instructed him to search in his saddlebag and withdraw the small casket. He had not handed that to Abigail with Alys's other few belongings. He wished to give her the contents himself. Then he saw his daughter turning and riding over to him.

He dismounted and handed her down. Although Alys shrank from the idea that she must leave him and England, no sign of it showed in her countenance. She must be strong or she would break down.

They walked a little on the river bank, then stood side by side, their hands clasped tight. Suddenly, Lord Symons let go and withdrew the casket from inside the folds of his cloak. He held it out to his beloved daughter.

'Alys, I want you to have this,' he said. 'It is yours by right.'

'Father!'

She recognised the silver casket with awe. It was the one which always rested in a secret drawer of the small dressing-table in Lady Symons' bedchamber, locked away from prying eyes. Alys drew in her breath as her father unlocked the casket.

'You know what this is, Alys?' he asked, bringing out the necklace.

'Yes, Father.'

Suddenly, before her dazzled eyes, the Throxton sapphires twinkled in the morning light.

'Why have you brought them here?'

'I have brought them for you. They are your heritage. Every Throxton bride must wear them. They are our family's most prized possession. Your mother has only worn them twice, once when she wedded me and, once, to celebrate our dear Queen's coronation.'

Lord Symons took the necklace from the casket and fastened it carefully about Alys's neck. The blue stones flashed and sparkled in the rosy tight.

'They suit you very well,' he said, satisfied.

'But I cannot wear them now,' she said. 'You should take them back to safety, Father.'

She was happy and sad all at once.

'No, Alys. No, indeed. You are my only daughter and you deserve them. How the stones match your eyes! You are so beautiful. And ready to take a husband you love.'

He kissed her on both cheeks and his eyes were bright with tears. Alys was overwhelmed. She could hardly speak.

They stood for a moment then she said, 'May I show Nicholas?'

He smiled at her girlishness and handed her the little casket.

'Do with them what you want, daughter. I told you, they are yours.'

'What about Mother? She will think I stole them.'

'No, she will not. She will learn the truth from my own lips. They are not hers to give, but mine. And there are other things to take, too, which Nicholas knows of. I have furnished him with a dowry, so you need not be ashamed. It is already on its way to the coast with a small escort. He has told me what time you sail and where you are bound. One of his father's ships is waiting for you.'

'You are so good, Father,' she replied, feeling tears prick her eyes.

'Do not weep, daughter, or you will start me, too. Say my farewells to young Merson, who will soon be my son-in-law. Take care you send messages to me.'

Taking her in his arms, he hugged her close to his chest.

'God speed, Alys!'

Suddenly, her father let her go and swiftly strode back to his horse. Alys watched him mount, turn his horse's head and gallop off into the forest. It was then she gave vent to her true grief.

*   *   *

The upstairs room of the inn was the best that the coastal village could provide. Although the wind coming off the sea was gusting loud, there was a good fire and only a little smoke blowing down the chimney. It was a large, cosy room with a bedroom off to the left under the eaves.

Nicholas had both surprised and delighted her when he had ordered Abby to unpack the small chest his mother had sent. Inside lay a bride's gown, fashioned in lace. Butterflies and birds had been worked into it with coloured silks, and gold braid had been plaited into its skirt.

' 'Twas my mother's wedding dress,' he said. 'It is a trifle old-fashioned, but you are not offended, are you, dearest Alys?'

'Indeed I am not. 'Tis wonderful, Nicholas, but should we unpack this now before we take ship?'

'Oh, Alys.'

He laughed.

'We have spent a day and night on the road unwedded. I promise you tonight, at this inn, we shall be wed.'

Her colour rose at the thought. Before, she had been afraid that Alexander Huston would catch up with them. Now she had confidence to think of other things.

'Tonight, dear Alys, we shall be husband and wife.'

'How?' she asked, not thinking of anything but him.

'We are to meet Tom, are we not?'

She nodded. He had told her that Tom would be joining them, but she had believed it would be on the ship.

'He will be here soon to perform the sweetest office he has yet undertaken. But, secretly.'

He looked very serious.

'No-one must know or we are lost. The innkeeper and his wife have been told we are merchants.'

'I understand,' she nodded.

But it was already very late into the night when the innkeeper brought the news that their visitor had arrived. Before Nicholas went down to meet his brother, he told Alys to make herself ready and Abby immediately set to.

'Oh, mistress,' Abby said a few minutes later, 'I think you are the fairest bride I have ever set eyes on.'

The old-fashioned dress fitted very well and Abby cried out with pleasure at the bride she made, even more so when Alys bid her unlock the silver casket. Alys felt Abby's fingers tremble as she fastened the sapphires about her neck and Alys was sorry that her maid had nothing as beautiful. It was then she gave Abby the tiny golden locket she usually wore.

'Thank you, mistress Alys, 'tis the most beautiful present I have ever had.'

The maid's eyes were full of tears.

'Here, let me fasten it,' Alys said, satisfied. 'And you must put on your best, Abby, too.'

'I have little with me, mistress, which would suit a wedding.'

'Then we must find you something of mine,' Alys said, rummaging in another chest. 'Here, take this.'

'But 'tis too good for me, miss,' Abby gasped.

'Nonsense, you must look beautiful at my wedding, and for Peter.'

The girl blushed. Some moments later, the men were knocking at the chamber door to see if they were ready. Tom, although he looked pale and tired, embraced Alys warmly. When he took off his cloak, he put on a white stole, which had been concealed beneath his sober doublet.

Nicholas had unpacked and was wearing a lace-decorated jerkin, ornamented with seed pearls, which Alys much admired. He wore an elegant golden chain about his neck and looked very much the bridegroom. He had even seen to it that Peter was dressed in embroidered livery, too. The ceremony was both beautiful and brief. They could not risk their vows being overheard. Afterwards, as Alys and Nicholas kneeled before Tom to receive his blessing, their hearts were full. When they rose and kissed, Tom turned to their servants.

'My brother tells me that Peter would wed Miss Abigail.'

The servant inclined his head.

'Then step ye forward and I will bless that union also.'

It was with the greatest delight that Alys and Nicholas watched their servants wedded. Then the four embraced warmly. Afterwards, Alys bid Abby to go with her new husband and take some time for herself.

As Alys prepared herself for her wedding night in the adjoining chamber, Tom and Nicholas sat in deep conversation. It was only when she heard her husband call her in that Alys entered, wrapped in her mantle. Nicholas was as pale as Tom, who was standing beside him, holding his shoulder.

'He will not come with us, Alys. Tomorrow he returns to Merson.'

'But you must come. You must, Tom!'

She could see how wounded Nicholas was and could understand the terrible fear in his eyes.

'I must not, sweet sister,' Tom said. 'I have my flock to shepherd.'

He turned and looked out of the window into the darkness.

'And my destiny to face.'

'It will be death!' Nicholas cried.

'Then so be it, brother. I was born to be a priest and a priest I will die. I cannot run away from England like some whipped dog.'

'Then I must go with you!'

'No, brother, you have a wife now. You must save yourself and her. God grant that when the Catholic faith is accepted once more in England, we may all meet again.'

He embraced them both and the newly-weds could see that nothing would persuade him.

'I will rest here tonight and early in the morning will return to Merson. I will tell our parents the happy news.'

He took his brother's hand and held it. Then he kissed Alys on the cheek.

'Do not cry, my sister. If we do not meet again in this life, I trust we shall meet in Heaven. Good-night!' He smiled, adding, 'And sleep well.'

The sleep they enjoyed that night was truly the sweetest Alys had ever taken. So many things ran through her mind as she lay with her head on Nicholas's chest. All thoughts of the evil she had experienced at the hands of her mother were far from her mind. Nicholas had cried out in dismay when he had seen her bruised flesh and he had kissed all those poor places, vowing she would never again be ill-used.

She had thought of Tom then and prayed that Huston would not take him, and of her lonely father and her hopes of seeing him again.

In the light of her wedding dawn, she raised herself up and looked upon the handsome face of her sleeping husband. Now she was a married woman, she was privy to all his secrets. Alys laid her head in the hollow of his shoulder again and rested, her full lips curving into a satisfied smile, which sprang from deep inside her.

She knew with all a woman's instinct that their enforced exile from England would be bearable, even unto death, as long as their love remained.

We hope you have enjoyed this Large Print book. Other Chivers Press or G.K. Hall & Co. Large Print books are available at your library or directly from the publishers.

For more information about current and forthcoming titles, please call or write, without obligation, to:

Chivers Press Limited
Windsor Bridge Road
Bath BA2 3AX
England
Tel. (01225) 335336

OR

G.K. Hall & Co
295 Kennedy Memorial Drive
Waterville
Maine 04901
USA

All our Large Print titles are designed for easy reading, and all our books are made to last.